DIS ■■■■■■■■■■ ARD

D0866351

BL— 4.1
AR— 8.0

HEIDI LANG

RULES
OF THE
RUFF

AMULET BOOKS
NEW YORK

For Sean, who taught me to seek adventure.
I'm forever grateful that I get to explore these
strange trails with you.

Library of Congress Cataloging-in-Publication Data
Names: Lang, Heidi, author.
Title: Rules of the Ruff / by Heidi Lang.
Description: New York: Amulet Books, [2018] | Summary: Jessie, twelve, copes with what promised to be a long, boring summer with relatives by becoming apprentice to Wes, a grouchy neighborhood dog walker, who is facing new competition. Identifiers: LCCN 2017054250 | ISBN 9781419731372 (hardcover with jacket) Subjects: | CYAC: Dog walking—Fiction. | Dogs—Fiction. | Summer employment—Fiction. | Cousins—Fiction. Classification: LCC PZ7.1.L3436 Rul 2018 | DDC [Fic]—dc23

Text copyright © 2018 Heidi Lang
Illustrations copyright © 2018 Julia Bereciartu
Book design by Alyssa Nassner

Amulet Books are available at special discounts when purchased in quantity for premiums and promotions as well as fundraising or educational use. Special editions can also be created to specification. For details, contact specialsales@abramsbooks.com or the address below.

Amulet Books® is a registered trademark of Harry N. Abrams, Inc.

ABRAMS The Art of Books
195 Broadway, New York, NY 10007

"WHOEVER SAID DIAMONDS
ARE A GIRL'S BEST FRIEND
NEVER OWNED A DOG."

—Author unknown

CHAPTER 1

Jessie knew persistence was the key to getting anything she wanted. She liked to picture herself as a trickle of water, slowly and endlessly dripping, wearing down stones and filling oceans.

"How many times have I told you no, you irritating child?" Wes asked her. His tone was gruff and discouraging, but at least he'd opened his front door again at her knock. That was a good sign.

"I don't keep track of things like that." Jessie smiled her best smile, the one she'd seen her dad use whenever he needed something. "I only focus on the positive. And right now, I'm positive that you're getting tired of telling me no."

Wes ran two fingers up and down the deep groove between his eyebrows, as if he thought he might be able to smooth it out. He was a funny-looking man, what with those bushy eyebrows and that too-wide nose, his gray-blond hair long enough that it brushed his shoulders and floated around his head. "I work alone. *Alone*," he said, drawing out the word.

"You can still work alone. I'd just come along and help out."

"Do you even understand the meaning of the word 'alone'?"

"Of course I do. But in this case, I think I could be a huge asset to you."

"'Asset,' huh?" His scowl twitched around the edges. "That's a pretty fancy word for a kid. How old are you?"

Jessie's heart leapt at the question. Usually, he'd have slammed the door in her face by now. "Twelve," she said.

"And what's your name again?"

"Jessie. Jessie Jamison."

He winced. "Terrible alliteration."

"My dad's name is James Jamison."

"Then he should have known better."

"That's not a very nice thing to say," Jessie said.

"Yeah, well, I'm not a very nice man. And frankly, you're not a very nice child. A nice child would have gone away by now. A nice child would have listened when I said no the first, oh, seven hundred times."

Jessie nodded slowly. "OK," she said. "OK, I'm probably not nice. But I'm a hard worker, and I really, really love dogs. And I'm not even asking you to pay me. Just take me on, just for a week, and see how it goes." She needed this job. Without it, her summer would be an endless stretch of desolation, a desert island with nothing to do and no one to do it with.

"A week, eh?" Wes hooked his thumbs in the elastic of his hip pack and studied her. "Don't you have friends to bother? Or video games to play? Or whatever it is you kids do these days?"

"No."

"No?" He raised his bushy eyebrows. "Elaborate."

Jessie took a deep breath. "I'm visiting my cousin for the summer, and right now, she hates me. I don't have any other friends out here. And I don't really like video games; it's too much sitting around."

"I've noticed you have trouble staying in one place."

Jessie paused, her weight on her left foot. She realized she'd been hopping from foot to foot this whole time and carefully lowered her right foot to the ground. "I can stand still if I need to. If it is important for the job."

Wes sighed. "Look, kid, the whole reason I became a dog walker was so I wouldn't have to deal with people. And you are a particularly irritating person."

Jessie couldn't argue with that. Still, she wasn't ready to give up, not when they'd just had their longest conversation yet. He was definitely weakening; she just needed to give him one more good push.

He started to close the door in her face.

"Wait!" Jessie moved fast, sticking her foot in the way. "You at least have to admit I've been *doggedly* determined."

He stared at her, the door falling open again. "Please tell me you did not just say that."

"If you give me a job, I'll stop *hounding* you."

"Please stop." He kept his mouth in a firm upside-down U, but his blue eyes twinkled, and Jessie knew he wanted to laugh. "If I take you on, will you stop these terrible dog puns?"

"Absolutely. I'll put them on *paws*."

He rubbed the groove between his eyebrows again

and muttered, "Can't believe I'm doing this." Dropping his hand, he looked Jessie up and down. "Fine. Fine, irritating small person, I will take you on."

Triumph surged through Jessie. She'd done it. She would get to meet not one, not two, but probably a dozen dogs. Maybe more. How many dogs did Wes walk? It didn't matter; she would love them all, and they would love her back. They wouldn't abandon her or give her that look like her very existence was too annoying for words. "Thank you, thank you—"

He held up his hand, stopping her. "I'll take you on . . . but only on one condition."

Jessie swallowed. "Yes?"

Wes smiled, and suddenly Jessie was filled with a sense of foreboding, like she'd just stepped in a deep sucking pool of mud. He leaned toward her. "You'll have to master the Rules of the Ruff."

"Wh-what are those?"

"They are the code I live my life by. You'll learn to think like a dog, to act like a dog, to be a dog." He straightened. "Come back tomorrow morning. Seven sharp. Your training starts then." He disappeared back into his house, closing the door with a final-sounding click.

Jessie stared at that closed door, her eyes tracing the peeling white paint.

Seven in the morning, in the summer. Did he have any idea how early that was? She slowly walked down the three steps to the sidewalk and turned left. Maybe Wes was just trying to discourage her. Well, it wouldn't work. She could get up early, if she had to. She could learn to be a dog, too. She would master these Rules of the Ruff if it was the last thing she did.

As she followed the sidewalk, she pushed her bangs off her forehead, glad she'd chopped her thick, curly hair short before coming out here to Elmsborough, Ohio, for the summer. It was almost ten in the morning now, and the day's heat had already begun to build. She imagined the heat as a large, soggy blanket that someone was holding just above her head. Even though it wasn't touching her yet, she could feel the threat of it being dropped on her.

Jessie made another left. Up ahead was Elm Park, her favorite part of this whole place. She loved how big it was, so huge she couldn't see the circular pond at the far end. Most of the park was flat and grassy, surrounded by a winding trail lined with the elm trees that gave it its name. In the far corner stood a swing set and jungle gym that she and Ann used to play on, back when they were kids. Back when Ann was still fun. Back when she was still Ann and not Ann-*Marie*. Jessie scowled as she passed by the swings, then decided she'd wasted enough time thinking about her stupid cousin.

Her soccer ball was still crammed under the bushes where she'd hidden it. Jessie crouched low and dug it out, then tossed it from hand to hand. If she wanted to be a starter when school began, she needed to keep her skills sharp. It was hard, though; all her favorite drills required at least two people. If only Ann would . . . but no.

Jessie dropped the soccer ball, enjoying the sound it made as it crushed the grass, that crinkly noise, so full of promise. She rolled her shoulders and did a few quick lunges and stretches. Then she picked up the ball and started juggling with it. She eased into it, hitting the ball first with her feet, working it up to her knees, and then finally bouncing it up and off her head.

"Not bad."

Jessie whirled around. The ball fell from her head, bouncing to the ground and rolling until it was stopped by a sneaker-clad foot. Jessie's eyes traced that foot up. White sock. Brown shin. Black shorts.

A tall boy with huge brown eyes smiled down at her.

"What do you want?" Jessie demanded.

His grin slipped a little. "Well, I guess I was hoping you were looking for a partner."

"A partner?"

"You know, for soccer drills."

"Soccer drills." Jessie eyed him. He looked like he was in good enough shape. Still. "How do I know you don't suck? I mean, I don't want to be saddled with someone terrible."

"I don't suck. Watch this." He took off his faded baseball cap. His thick black hair was even curlier than Jessie's, and he shoved it back from his face and stuffed his hat over it backward, then scooped up her soccer ball. He dropped it, catching it on one outstretched foot and balancing it there. Then he bounced it up and ducked under it, catching it on the top of his head and balancing it there for a few seconds, too. He bounced it again, catching it on his left shoulder, then his right, then his knees and thighs. That took control, serious control. Jessie was impressed in spite of herself.

He grinned at her and finally let the ball drop down. "Pretty good, right?"

She scowled. She didn't like his cocky attitude. "Do you actually know how to play soccer or just a bunch of fancy tricks?"

"I know how to play." He sounded hurt.

"Oh yeah? Well, what position?"

"Center forward."

"How many goals have you scored?"

"Total, or per game?"

Jessie thought about it for a second. "Per game."

"My best game, I scored eight, with two assists."

That wasn't bad. Jessie decided she'd never tell him her own best record, which was only five goals in a game with three assists. "Fine," she said reluctantly. "I guess you can play with me."

"Well, how do I know *you* don't suck?"

Jessie noticed his incisors were a little longer and sharper than most people's. They dimpled his bottom lip when he smiled, giving him a mischievous look, like a fox. "I don't suck," she said. "And I don't need to show off to prove it, either. We can play one-on-one, and I'll show you."

"Confident. I like it. I'm Max, by the way." He stuck out his hand.

"Jessie." She shook it, feeling strangely grown up.

He squinted at her a second, like he was sizing her up, then nodded. "All right, let's do this."

Max ended up winning, but not by much. Still, Jessie hated to lose to anyone. "One more," she said, wiping the sweat from her brow with the sleeve of her T-shirt. "Winner takes all."

Max laughed, his brown eyes crinkling at the edges, almost closing. "OK, one more—"

"Jessie!"

Jessie turned, and her heart plummeted. Her cousin was stalking toward her through the grass, her narrow face twisted in annoyance. Behind her trailed a tall girl with long, chestnut-brown hair and overly glossy lips. Those lips curled in a smile at the sight of Jessie. It was the kind of smile a cat would give a small, injured bird, and Jessie shivered and looked away from her. If she ignored Loralee, maybe Loralee would leave her alone.

"Hi Ann." Jessie nodded at her cousin. "What's up?"

"It's Ann-Marie," Ann said firmly. "And Mom is furious you've been gone so long. You'd better come home now."

Loralee looked Jessie up and down. "I see your dad is still lending you his shirts. How . . . nice."

"Shut up, Loralee." Jessie tugged self-consciously at her overlarge T-shirt, very aware of Max standing behind her.

"Shut up, Loralee," the other girl mocked. And then her eyes slid past Jessie and widened. "Oh, sorry, I didn't realize you actually made a friend." She wiggled her fingers at Max. "Hello."

"Hey," Max said, his voice deeper than it had been a moment ago.

"I'm Loralee."

"Max," he said, smiling his fox smile.

"Are you new? I've never seen you before. I'm sure I'd remember if I had."

"Loralee, we should go," Ann whispered, but Loralee ignored her.

His smile widened. "Yeah, I moved here about a month ago with my mom."

"Hmm. Well it was nice of you to play with Jessie," Loralee said, like Max was doing her such a big favor.

"I wasn't being nice." Max's smile dropped away, and he looked annoyed. Jessie could have hugged him. "We were having a good game."

"Oh yeah?" Loralee glanced at Jessie, her eyes hardening. "Well, I'm sorry we interrupted, then."

"Nah, it was over. He's pretty good, but I'm better." Max grinned and punched Jessie in the shoulder. "Right?"

There was a moment of stunned silence. Jessie felt frozen in it, until Loralee's squeal of laughter shattered the ice and there was nothing but fire—fire in Jessie's cheeks, fire in her ears, fire behind her eyes.

"Oh . . . my . . . *god!*" Loralee shrieked. "He thinks you're a boy!" She turned to Ann. "Isn't that just the funniest thing?"

Ann looked uncomfortable. "I guess so," she said.

Jessie just pushed past them all and started home. She didn't want them to see her cry.

"Uh, sorry, Jessie," Max called after her, sounding awkward. "I didn't mean . . . I mean, I didn't know. Um, see you around later? You know, for our rematch?"

Jessie kept walking, but she lifted one arm in a wave,

as if it didn't matter to her. Then she let her arm fall. It felt heavy. Her whole body felt heavy, but she forced her legs to move, move, move, and as soon as she turned the corner, she ran all the way back to her cousin's house. She didn't feel like a trickle of water anymore. She felt like the stones beneath the water, worn away. Beaten.

CHAPTER 2

Beep. Beep. Beep.

Jessie turned over, pulling the blankets over her head.

Beep-beep. Beep-beep.

She pressed her ears into her pillow, chasing sleep.

Beep beep beep! Beep beep beep!

"Turn that thing off!"

Jessie bolted upright. She blinked around the darkened room, blearily making out her cousin's annoyed face on the other side, and between them, growing increasingly angry, her small white alarm clock. Jessie turned it off.

"Thank you," Ann huffed. "Why did you set an alarm? And so early?"

"I have things to do," Jessie said, rubbing the sleep from her eyes.

"What could you possibly have to do today?"

"Like I'm going to tell you." Jessie got up and pulled her suitcase out from under her cot, rummaging around for something to wear. "Go back to sleep."

"Jessie . . . Mom's not going to like you sneaking out in the morning."

Jessie found a shirt and a pair of gray sweatpants and turned to face her cousin. "Are you going to tell her?"

Ann bit her lip. She was lying on her side, her head propped on her hand, her blond hair a tangle around her head. Jessie remembered all the summer nights they'd spent in mirroring poses like that, gossiping, telling stories, making plans. Things had started changing last summer, but they'd still had fun together. Up until that moment, that excruciating, humiliating moment that Jessie refused to think about.

This summer, though, Ann was like a stranger to her—a stranger she didn't particularly like. Ann was only two years older, but now it felt like an impossible gap, and Jessie could picture it growing wider and wider, as if her cot was sliding away from Ann's bed, from Ann's side of the room, from Ann's life.

"No," Ann said finally. "Go do whatever it is. But if you get in trouble, I'm not going to back you up, either."

Jessie snorted. "Don't worry, Ann-*Marie*," she said, emphasizing the name. "I remember you don't like to stick up for me. Not anymore."

Ann flinched. "Jess, I'm sorry. About Loralee. I know she can seem a little . . . but she means well, really."

"No, she doesn't." Loralee had spent the rest of the day at their house yesterday, and Jessie had been forced to endure the other girl's taunts, since Aunt Beatrice had forbidden her from leaving the house again. Dinner had been particularly painful. "Loralee is a mean girl. And you're . . ." She stopped, took a deep breath. "You're worse. You're supposed to be my cousin."

"I *am* your cousin." Ann's voice quavered.

"Not really. Not anymore." Jessie got dressed and left the room before more words could come pouring out. They didn't make her feel any better, and she didn't want anything to ruin this morning.

She ran her fingers through her messy hair, all thoughts of Ann fading as she slipped out the back door, shutting it softly behind her. Her aunt and uncle would be waking up by now, and the last thing she wanted was for one of them to stop her.

It was already light out, the sky a faded blue. Jessie shivered. She knew it would be hot and muggy in a few hours, but right now she was wishing she'd worn a sweatshirt.

When she reached the hedge that lined her aunt and uncle's yard, she paused, remembering how she'd been staring at it the day she first saw Wes and his pack of dogs. It was after her first big fight with Ann, and the summer stretched ahead of her, long and boring and impossibly lonely. That day, as she sat outside listening to the whirring of bicycles and cars hurrying to better places, this hedge had seemed like an inescapable boundary.

Until a flurry of dog barking split the quiet of the afternoon.

Jessie ran her hand over the hedge's prickly top,

recalling that moment, the moment she'd finally figured out exactly what she should do this summer.

It had been almost a week ago today.

"Bear, you knock that off, you hear me?" a man yelled as a pack of five dogs pulled him around the corner, their leashes clipped to a hip pack he wore slung low on his waist. He wasn't very tall, but his arms were well-muscled, and underneath his soft stomach Jessie could tell he used to be in pretty good shape. Probably an athlete before he got old.

"I said stop, Bear! That squirrel is long gone." The man tugged at one of his leashes, and Bear, a large black mutt with lopsided ears, gave one last bark and then lapsed into happy silence, his tongue lolling out of his mouth.

The Australian shepherd next to Bear made a little noise. "Don't you start, Presto." The man clucked his tongue, flicked the leashes like they were a horse's reins, and got all the dogs moving in formation. It was like magic. Jessie couldn't take her eyes off it, all those dogs walking together, looking so happy. She *had* to go see them.

She leapt over the hedge and jogged toward them. "Excuse me, can I pet your dogs?"

"No," the man said, not bothering to look at her. "Go away."

His dogs shot her curious glances, and one of them, a yellow Labrador wearing a pink harness, darted over to lick her hands.

"Sweetpea, you stop that." He tugged at the Lab, but

Sweetpea had decided to sit, and now all the dogs moved around in a jumble, ignoring the man and his curses as he struggled to straighten them out and get them moving again.

Jessie snuck a quick pat of Sweetpea's soft head before he pulled the dog away. "This is why I don't stop to talk," he snarled at Jessie as he adjusted all the tangled leashes.

"Are you a professional dog walker?"

"No, these are all mine."

"Really?"

He raised his eyebrows. "Sure, kid, and I have a bridge to sell you, too."

"You sell bridges?"

He sighed. Sweetpea inched closer to Jessie. "Yes, I walk dogs. Professionally. See this?" He jerked a thumb at his hip pack. "Do you see people casually walking their dogs wearing one of these beauties?"

"Um, no . . ."

"No is right. Now, I doubt you'd go harass a fireman in the middle of hosing down a burning building, would you?"

"Firefighter," Jessie said automatically. "You're supposed to use the gender-neutral term." Her father had drilled that into her head.

He scowled. "Like I was saying, you'd notice his uniform and that he was busy and leave him alone."

"Or her."

His mouth twisted. "I can see you have honed the fine art of being annoying to an impressive level."

"Thanks!" Jessie beamed.

He shook his head. "Come on, dogs." He started walking but was brought up short once again. His forehead wrinkled and he growled, "Sweetpea, come."

Sweetpea must have known she was in trouble; she reluctantly stopped inching toward Jessie and allowed herself to be herded along with the others.

Jessie had watched them until they disappeared around the corner. *When you're a little older, we'll get a dog . . .* Her mother had promised her, but that was before she got sick. And after, all her promises had scattered like dry leaves in the fall, crumbling to dust. After, Jessie had been afraid to ask her dad about it, in case he crumbled, too. But seeing that strange man with his magical pack of dogs made her realize here was her chance: She might not have her own dog, but she could borrow one. She could borrow a whole pack.

She'd decided then and there that she would become a dog walker, too. She'd get that grumpy old guy to take her on as an assistant, and then she'd spend her whole summer surrounded by dogs.

Jessie gave herself a little shake, letting the memory fade, but the excitement filling her stomach remained. Excitement and a little bit of nervousness. She thought of those emotions as peanut butter and jelly, so sticky it was hard to tell where the line between them was.

Picking up her pace, she jogged the remaining blocks to Wes's house.

Wes sat on his front porch, a steaming mug in his

hand. He wore a red-and-orange plaid flannel shirt over his normal white tank top, and his eyes narrowed on Jessie as she ran up. "You're late."

"You said seven. It's seven."

Wes tapped his wristwatch, then held it out to her.

Jessie squinted at it. It read 7:03 A.M. "Your watch is fast," she decided.

He made a show of sipping from his mug and didn't answer.

"Coffee?" Jessie asked.

"No, green tea."

"Green tea?" Jessie made a face. "Don't all adults drink coffee?"

"Coffee is a crutch. I don't believe in it." Wes took another sip.

"You don't believe in coffee?"

He sighed and put his mug down on a little ceramic coaster on his top step. "We need to establish some ground rules. And the first one is no questions."

"Is that one of the Rules of the Ruff?" Jessie asked excitedly.

"What did I tell you about questions?"

"Not to ask them?"

"Is that another question?" he demanded.

Jessie thought about it. "Maybe?" She grinned.

Wes rubbed the furrow between his eyebrows, muttering to himself. Jessie caught the words "irritating" and "child." Then he stood up. "Let's get this over with. Come."

"What about your mug?"

"No questions!"

Jessie followed Wes to his car, sparing one more glance at the mug sitting lost and alone on the top step. It made her think of Ann, and she looked away quickly.

"You're not sitting in the front," Wes said. "So just get that idea out of your head right now. Kids ride in back."

"Is that another one of those Ruff Rules?" Jessie asked as she climbed into the back, disturbing a layer of dog fur. It rose in a cloud around her, settling into her hair and clothes as she fastened her seat belt. She wrinkled her nose but didn't bother trying to brush it off. It would be a wasted effort.

"Rules of the Ruff, and no. This is just my own personal rule." Wes started the car and backed jerkily out of his driveway. "The first house isn't far, it's walkable distance. But this way I can get to the others without stopping back."

He made a left at the end of the street, then another left. They were heading in the direction of the candy store, Jessie noted. She purposely didn't think of the park, where they were also heading. She never wanted to see Max again. It would be too embarrassing. And then she remembered. "Oh no," she groaned.

"What?"

"My soccer ball. I left it . . . never mind." Jessie tried not to picture her ball sitting there, all abandoned in the middle of the park. Or worse, stolen by someone else. She would have to swing by the park again, after all. "What's the first Rule, then? Of the Ruff?" she asked, trying to distract herself.

"Rule Number One: If you have calm, confident energy, you can do anything. Dogs respect calm, confident energy. And if you don't have it, fake it."

Jessie worked his words through her mind. "I'm not sure I understand," she admitted as Wes pulled into a driveway. The house was a cheerful mint green with a wide, friendly porch that wrapped around the front.

"Well then, you won't pass this first test, and that'll be that."

"You mean, this is a test?"

"Of course it's a test."

"But that's not fair."

"Isn't it? You pass, and I continue to teach you. You fail?" He shrugged, then got out of the car.

Jessie's stomach tightened. She had to pee, but she knew this wasn't the time. It was like right before a big soccer game. It was just nerves. Still, as she followed Wes to the side of the house and stared at the large "Beware of Dog" sign hung on the tall wooden fence, she began to think that it wasn't just nerves. No, she really had to pee.

"What kind of dog is this?"

Wes flashed her a grin. "Are you familiar with pit bulls?"

"A little." Jessie swallowed nervously, remembering all the stories she'd heard of pit bulls mauling people, of their jaws locking when they bit down, so even in death they couldn't be opened.

"Most of what you've heard is a lie. They are usually very sweet and loving dogs." Wes handed her a worn green leash.

"U-usually?" Jessie clenched the leash, feeling it dig into her palm. "What about this one?"

"His name is Angel."

"And is that an appropriate name for him?" Jessie's heart hammered in her ears, and she thought she could hear something growling on the other side of the fence. Something big.

"Not really," Wes said, chuckling. "Now, for this first test, I want you to go in there and leash him. Be careful, he jumps. And remember the first Rule. You need to be calm, confident. Otherwise Angel won't respect you. And he doesn't respond well if you don't have his respect."

"Wait, what does that mean? 'Doesn't respond well'?"

"I told you, no questions."

"But that's just very vague, and—"

Wes pulled on the gate latch and shoved Jessie through, then yanked the gate shut behind her.

"H-hey!" she sputtered.

"Just do your job," Wes called from the safe side of the fence.

"My job." Jessie turned nervously, but she was alone in the small grass yard. A massive doghouse dominated the space, but its entrance appeared dark and empty. At her feet were the remains of a rubber toy, ripped in half, as well as the carcasses of several unfortunate tennis balls and a few stuffed animals. "Uh, I don't think he's here,"

Jessie said hopefully. She nudged one of the toys with her sneaker, flipping it onto its back. A teddy bear stared back at her, the head badly bitten, stuffing oozing out of the neck. It had only one eye.

A low growl raised the hairs on the back of Jessie's neck. She lifted her head. And then she realized the dog wasn't in his doghouse. Angel was right behind her.

Jessie turned, but she felt like she was moving in a dream, all slow motion and thick gravy air. Angel stood only a few feet away, his fur a glossy brown, his eyes wide and deep. He was huge, his chest twice as wide as Jessie's, his leg muscles bulging.

Angel growled again, his lips pulling back to show off his teeth, and Jessie took a step back, then another, holding the leash in front of her like it was a shield. "H-hey, Angel. G-good boy."

Angel barked, and Jessie dropped the leash and scrambled for the gate latch. It wouldn't open. "Wes! Wes, let me out!" She pounded at the gate.

"You need to face this, kid."

She turned and faced Angel. It was not an improvement. "He's not happy to see me!"

"Remember the first Rule."

"I don't. I forgot it. I'm not ready!"

Wes snorted. "Not ready. I don't believe in this 'not ready' nonsense. Do you think dogs need time to prepare? No. They act, or they do not act. You must achieve the mind of a dog to properly walk a dog."

"What does that even mea—*aagh!*"

Angel's leg muscles bunched, and then he was airborne, his front paws catching Jessie right in the chest and knocking her to the ground. Jessie landed so hard all the air whooshed out of her lungs, and she was left gasping with the pit bull on top of her, those teeth inches from her face.

CHAPTER 3

Jessie couldn't breathe. Angel's paws were crushing the life out of her, and she had a face full of dog breath and saliva. All she could see were teeth, lots and lots of teeth, plenty to get the job done. She closed her eyes. This was it. She was going to die beneath the paws of a dog.

Slurp!

Jessie's eyes shot open.

Slurp. Slurp. Angel's tongue caught Jessie across her whole face and nose, leaving them cold and wet and sticky. It was completely disgusting but better than having her face chomped. Probably.

Jessie squirmed until she managed to free herself from under Angel. She wiped her face on her sleeve as she sat up, uncomfortably aware of the dog's steady, unblinking gaze.

"You still alive, kid?" Wes called.

"Yes," Jessie said. "Barely."

"Oh, good. I was not looking forward to the paperwork involved otherwise."

Jessie scowled. "Well, I'm glad I didn't inconvenience you." She stood, and so did Angel.

Jessie eyed the dog. She felt bruised all over; the last thing she wanted was a repeat flying tackle. "Sit," she ordered.

Angel ignored her command completely, his tongue lolling. Was he laughing at her? She took a deep breath, remembering the first Rule. Calm and confident. Too bad she didn't feel either of those things. Her hands still shook and she kept picturing Angel's teeth looming over her face.

Angel made a little whining noise, and Jessie's heart beat faster. She shook her arms out, letting her breath go. Calm and confident. Calm and confident. Repeating the words wasn't helping, so instead she pictured a great big redwood tree. She'd seen tons of them last year when her father picked up that lumber job in California. They had seemed so proud, like they would be there forever. Like the world could change around them, but they never would. Jessie liked that. She imagined herself as one of them, her feet as roots, her arms as branches, her body solid as wood.

She looked at Angel. "Sit."

Angel sat.

Relief made Jessie light-headed. It was working. "Stay." She took a step back and Angel stayed. "I'm a natural," she whispered. She felt as if she'd just scored the winning goal in a game.

She found her discarded leash a few feet away. Angel whined again, his tail kicking up dirt behind him, his large brown eyes fixed intently on the leash in Jessie's hands.

Here was the moment of truth. Jessie swallowed hard as she moved closer to Angel. Even sitting, the dog's head reached her waist, and there was no getting around those bulging muscles. Jessie held her breath as she leaned over him, moving her hands closer to that mouth to clip the leash onto Angel's metal-studded collar. Angel smiled up at her, still sitting patiently like the best dog in the world.

Tentatively, Jessie put out a hand and scratched behind Angel's left ear. He leaned his head into it, and she relaxed. "Aww, you're a friendly pit, aren't you?"

"Are you having a party in there, or what?" Wes asked. "Hurry it up, kid. The leashing is supposed to be the easy part. We still need to walk the dog."

Jessie rolled her eyes. The easy part? Yeah, right. Holding the leash tightly in both hands, she told Angel, "heel," and walked to the gate. Angel trotted obediently at her side, and Jessie knocked confidently at the gate.

"Is he leashed?" Wes asked.

"You bet."

"OK, hold on tight." The gate opened.

Angel gave Jessie one last loving look, his brown eyes wide and warm and innocent, and then *bam!* He shot through the open gate so fast he dragged Jessie through like a kite in a hurricane. Wes lunged forward to catch her, but Jessie was already past him and still moving fast, stumbling and sliding behind Angel as the dog sprinted down the street. She heard a loud crash and then even louder cursing and knew she was on her own.

"Ground yourself, kid!" Wes hollered. "Drop your

weight, bend your arms and knees. And for the love of dog, don't let go of that leash!"

Jessie's knuckles were white, her arms shaking. She couldn't drop her weight, couldn't bend her arms, could only run as Angel picked up speed, and the houses and yards and happy, carefree people blurred behind her. Jessie had never run so fast in her life. Not in any of her soccer practices, not even when they'd practiced sprints. Her world narrowed to the dog charging forward, the leash clutched desperately in her hand, and her legs turning over and over. She ran until she tasted blood in the back of her throat and her hands went numb, until her lungs burned and her legs ached, and then she ran some more.

And then Angel abruptly sat down. Jessie's arm jerked to a sudden stop, her feet carrying her a few steps before she was able to catch herself. Gasping, she put her hands on her knees, the leash digging into her left palm. She managed to take several deep, shaky breaths, her head pounding, before she straightened and glared down at the pit bull.

Angel panted, his whole tongue drooping out of his wide-open mouth.

"You," Jessie gasped, shaking her head at the dog. "You'd better be tired."

Angel stretched out on the sidewalk, his body moving with each panting breath.

"Yeah, I thought so." Jessie stretched her aching back and looked around.

They were in a nice neighborhood, the houses here all two or three stories tall with wide, green lawns and carefully manicured bushes. Jessie felt like she'd been running for hours, but it was probably more like fifteen minutes; it was still early and hardly anyone was out yet. Down the road, a man was enthusiastically washing his car, while two houses away, three little girls played jump rope next to a middle-aged woman reclining on a lounge chair, but otherwise it was quiet. There was no sign of Wes.

Jessie's heart sank. She didn't recognize any of this. She had no idea where they were, and worse, she wasn't actually sure which way they'd come from. Angel had turned a few times, but Jessie hadn't been able to pay attention to where.

Angel stood abruptly. His ears pricked forward, lips pulled back.

"What are you doing?" Jessie asked nervously.

Angel let out a low, menacing growl. "Angel, s-stop." Jessie pulled at the leash, and then she heard it, too: Over the sound of Angel growling and the children playing and the man spraying his car, someone was yelling.

Jessie looked up. A dog was running toward them, dragging a leash behind it like a cape. Its ears were flattened back against its head, but even from this distance Jessie could tell it was a German shepherd, a big one, its dark eyes fixed on Angel.

Angel lunged forward, yanking Jessie along. "Angel, no! Stop! Heel! Sit!" Jessie wheezed and panted and tried to yank back on the leash, but she couldn't stop Angel's determined sprint. She glimpsed a tree up ahead, and in a last effort, she threw her free arm out and caught it, clinging like a koala as the pull from Angel slammed her against the trunk. The momentum swung Angel around just as the other dog leapt, the two dogs barely missing each other.

The German shepherd landed, then spun gracefully to face Angel again. Angel snarled and lunged, slamming Jessie harder against the tree. She heard a car screech to a halt, and in the corner of her vision, she could see Wes running, not even bothering to shut his car door. He still wouldn't reach them in time. As the other dog leapt right at them, she braced herself for the impact.

And then a woman in hot-pink capris was there, thrusting herself in front of Jessie and catching the German shepherd mid-leap. She twisted, rolling the dog away from Jessie and Angel and coming up to her feet with a firm grip on the dangling leash.

Jessie's jaw dropped and she almost let go of a snarling Angel, but by then Wes was there. He grabbed Angel by the collar and hauled him back. "Sit," he said, with such authority Jessie found her own legs collapsing. He spared her a glance. "I wasn't talking to you. You don't need to sit."

"I . . . I'm good here," Jessie managed. Spots danced in her vision and she thought she might be sick. Wes had to open her hand and physically pull the leash from her numb fingers, and she leaned her head against the rough bark of the tree. "Thank you," she whispered.

He scowled down at her. "Don't thank me. This was my mistake. And *you*." He turned his scowl on the woman and her German shepherd. "What the heck was that?"

"I'm so, so sorry," the woman said, her gaze focused on Wes's shoulder like she couldn't stand to look him in the eyes. Jessie couldn't blame her; she had never felt anger like Wes's before. It reminded her of a space heater, throwing off heat and filling the air between them. "That was quick thinking, grabbing the tree like that," she told Jessie.

"Th-thank you," Jessie managed. She couldn't look away from the woman, from her lovely brown eyes and perfect cheekbones. With her black tank top and tight pink capris, she looked like a fashion model, but Wes seemed completely immune to her beauty.

"If you can't control your dog, you shouldn't—" He stopped abruptly, his eyes narrowing on the German shepherd. It gave Wes a wide doggie smile, looking nothing at all like the beast that had been lunging and snarling just seconds ago. "Is that Bruno?"

The woman flushed, and she took a step back. "Er, we'd better be on our way. Sorry again." And then she was jogging, the German shepherd trotting along at her side. Wes watched them go, a concerned furrow deepening between his eyebrows.

Jessie used the tree to stand, her legs shaking. "What's wrong?"

"I know that dog."

"And . . . that's a bad thing?"

"I *walk* that dog," he explained. "Except for this week, when his owner said he didn't need any walks. So, the question is, why is he being walked today by some amateur?" He didn't say another word as the woman and dog turned the corner and vanished from sight, but Jessie could practically feel his thoughts churning in his head like a vat of rocky road ice cream. She shivered.

CHAPTER 4

Jessie climbed into the back seat with Angel, feeling like a squeezed-up tube of old toothpaste. Wes tossed her a water bottle and a granola bar. "Th-thanks," she said. He said nothing, his lips pressed firmly together.

Jessie drained the whole bottle in three large gulps but couldn't bring herself to eat. Her stomach was still in knots, the water she'd chugged sloshing around inside her. It only got worse as they drove back to Angel's house, the dog's loud, panting breaths the only sounds in the car.

Wes pulled into the driveway and parked. He met her gaze in the rearview mirror. "Put Angel away and we'll talk."

Jessie's heart sank. She knew she hadn't made a very good showing of her first walk. She certainly hadn't been very calm or confident, and now she'd ruined everything. "Come, Angel." The pit bull followed her out of the car and over to the fence. Jessie slowly opened the gate and trudged through, shutting it behind her. When she unclipped Angel, he leaned forward and licked her hand, and Jessie scratched him behind the ear. "I forgive you," she whispered. Angel licked her once more, then turned and lumbered into his doghouse.

Jessie made sure the gate was firmly closed behind her. Then she opened the back door of Wes's car and got in. A million excuses filled her mouth, a million reasons why Wes should give her another chance, but they popped like soap bubbles in the face of his furious blue eyes. "I'm sorry," was all she could manage through the sudden lump in her throat.

His eyes widened. "Are you crying?"

"No," Jessie sniffled.

"Good. Because I have no use for crybabies. Do dogs cry? No. And neither do dog walkers."

Jessie sniffed again and wiped her eyes.

Wes sighed. "Besides, you did all right today, all things considered."

"R-really?"

He ran a finger down the now-familiar furrow between his bushy eyebrows. "Angel and Bruno . . . don't get along. I never walk them together. They react poorly."

Jessie let out a laugh that was also a half sob. "I hadn't noticed."

"I made a mistake, allowing you to take Angel out first," he continued, ignoring her comment. "I should have started with an easier dog, but, if I'm completely honest, I was hoping he would scare you and then you would leave me alone."

"I'm not scared," Jessie said quickly. Her hands were still trembling from the run-in with the other dog and she felt all weak and achy inside, but she wasn't scared of Angel.

"I know. So, I am willing to continue to teach you the Rules of the Ruff, if you would like to continue to learn."

Jessie's jaw dropped. "You are? Really?"

"I am already regretting this decision, but yes." He turned away from Jessie, clipped his seat belt into place, and backed out of the driveway. Jessie opened her mouth again, her head full of questions. "No questions," Wes snapped, before she had a chance to ask any of them.

"But—"

"No!"

"But why—"

"Definitely not."

"I just wondered—"

"I said no questions or the deal's off."

Jessie sighed. "Fine." She couldn't understand why he was still agreeing to teach her, but it didn't matter. What mattered was that she still had a job, and she'd get to spend her summer surrounded by dogs. She leaned back into the fur-covered seat and smiled. Then she ate the granola bar.

A few hours later, Jessie almost regretted Wes's change of heart. Her whole body ached, she felt like she was covered in dog slobber and fur, and she had never been so hungry. And the worst part? After her disastrous first walk with Angel, Wes wasn't letting her actually walk any of the dogs. No, her job was to help leash them and then to trot along behind him and pick up all the dog poop. Worst. Job. Ever.

"If you want to be a dog walker, you have to start at the bottom," Wes said cheerfully as Jessie cleaned up yet another pile.

"Ha ha, very funny. I'm glad you're so happy." Jessie tied a knot in the top of a plastic doggie bag and then held it away from her with two fingers. She glared at Sweetpea. "That was disgusting, by the way." The Lab gave her an innocent look, but Jessie wasn't buying it; that dog knew exactly what she'd done.

"Just glad I didn't have to clean that up," Wes chuckled. "This whole assistant thing is actually not so bad."

Jessie transferred her glare to him. She pictured herself chucking the poop bag right at his head. She could almost hear the satisfying *thwap* it would make when it caught him on the side of the face.

"Come on, dogs." Wes flicked the leashes, completely unaware of the danger he was in as he got his pack of five pups moving again.

It really was remarkable how each dog fell into place, the two Labs on his left, the two Border collies on his right, and the golden retriever trotting along right behind him. He made it look easy, like some kind of dance whose steps he'd mastered long ago. The dog pack they'd walked before this one had been the same way, each dog instinctively moving into position, until it seemed like Wes was barely walking them at all. She'd been too distracted by the cuteness of the dogs on that first walk, the magic of their formation, but this time she noticed that Wes kept a hand on each leash, that he was ready with a quick wrist flick or a sudden sharp noise to keep the pack in order.

Wes glanced at Jessie. "You still want to do this?"

"Yes!"

His mouth twitched. "OK. Just checking."

She didn't like cleaning up after the dogs, true, but Wes couldn't keep her on poop-scooping duty forever. She hoped. Maybe tomorrow she'd get to walk her own pack.

Would she ever be able to walk them like Wes did, though? Maybe after she learned all the Rules of the Ruff.

They finished the walk and Jessie helped load all the dogs back into the car. There wasn't a lot of space for her with five dogs crammed into the back seat, but Wes still wouldn't let her sit in front. Grumbling to herself, Jessie managed to squeeze in back. Immediately, Lady the black Lab took over most of her lap, and Sammy the golden retriever did his best to take over the rest until Jessie thought she might drown in dog.

Lady rested her little Lab head against Jessie's.

Not the worst way to go, Jessie thought as she stroked the Lab's silky ears.

They pulled up to the first house. Jessie unfolded herself and took the pair of Border collies out of the car, following Wes into the house. "These two get a special treat after each walk," Wes said, pointing out the jar on the counter full of fancy doggie biscuits.

"Lucky puppies," Jessie said. "Sit," she told Harley and Molly, calm and confident. They both sat, tails swishing across the carpet in identical blurs of excitement as Jessie handed each of them a biscuit.

"Lady stays outside," Wes instructed when they reached the next house. "You just want to double-check her water bowl." Jessie followed his orders, then gave Lady a quick pat before wedging herself back into the car.

"Sweetpea has a hidden key," Wes said as they pulled up to her house.

"A hidden key?"

"It means a key that's hidden."

"I guessed that already," Jessie muttered, face burning.

Wes grinned. "Just checking. Now, this isn't exactly a Rule of the Ruff, but it is something good to keep in mind." He got out of the car, and Jessie followed, Sweetpea trotting along next to her. "Most people keep a key hidden somewhere in their yard. Even the ones who've given me a copy most likely have a key stashed away somewhere."

"Really?"

"Absolutely." He walked around the house to the small yard in back. A back porch with a set of rickety stairs led up to a closed screen door. It looked a lot like the back of Wes's house, right down to the peeling paint on the railing. "Now, the best place to look is under anything that stands out. An empty pot? Probably has a key under it. A welcome mat is also a good place to look. Or in some cases," he picked up a small turtle statue half-hidden behind two potted plants, "it's hidden inside something like this." He flipped back the shell and Jessie could see a key glinting inside.

Wes gave her a sideways glance. "I hope you won't use your new knowledge for evil."

"Me?" Jessie widened her eyes.

Wes shook his head. "This may have been a mistake," he muttered, but when they drove to the last dog's house, he had Jessie search for the hidden key herself. She found it within a few minutes underneath an upside-down pot on the front porch.

"Nicely done," Wes said.

Jessie beamed at the compliment. "I feel like I'm preparing for a life of crime," she said, giving Sammy a good scratch behind the ears. "Why do so many people have a hidden key?"

"It beats having to remember one." Wes headed back to the car, Jessie trotting along at his heels.

"Do you have a hidden key?"

"None of your business, kid. Now, hop in."

Jessie hopped in. The back seat felt much larger, now that she was the only one in it. "Are we done?"

"Almost. I just need to pick up one more dog, and then I'll take you back." He drove a few minutes and then pulled into the driveway of a large brick house. It was the biggest house on the street, with an extravagant porch made of dark glossy wood and a white-painted gazebo peeking out from the spacious backyard.

"Wow, are these people rich?"

Wes scowled. "Mind your own business."

Jessie opened her car door, ready to go leash this new dog.

Wes's scowl deepened. "Stay."

"I'm not a dog," Jessie grumbled.

"I know. Believe me, I know. Dogs actually listen."

"I listen!"

"Not very well." He opened his car door. "I'll get this one. You just . . . just sit there." He got out, slapped at the dog fur that clung to his cargo shorts, and ran a quick hand through his messy hair. With a last tug at his shirt hem, he marched up the porch steps to the front door and knocked. Even from inside the car Jessie could hear the high-pitched barking that followed.

Jessie leaned into the front of the car to get a better look as a woman opened the door. She was pretty, at least for an older woman. She wore a simple pair of jeans and a sparkly blue top, her reddish-blond hair pulled into a fancy twist on top of her head and her earrings glinting in the sun like diamonds. Definitely rich.

The woman glanced back inside the house and said something, and the barking stopped. A few seconds later, a small dark gray shape hurtled itself from the house and leapt up, putting its front paws on Wes's leg. Jessie waited for him to push it off, to tell it "down" like he always did when a dog jumped on him, but he didn't. Instead he leaned down and scratched behind one of its pointed ears, his face strange.

It took Jessie a few seconds to realize why he looked so different. He was smiling. Actually smiling, showing teeth and everything, his blue eyes soft and gentle. *Creepy*, she decided. But as Wes walked toward the car, the dog at his side, she had to admit it *was* the cutest dog she'd ever seen. It was covered in thick dark fur, except for the white mask on its little narrow face and down its belly. With those pointed ears and the way it trotted along, it looked just like a husky, only smaller, maybe twenty pounds or so. Even though she'd never met one in person before, Jessie was pretty sure it was a Klee Klai.

Wes opened the copilot seat and the dog jumped in.

Jessie's jaw dropped. "You're letting the dog sit in front?"

Wes spared her a glance as he climbed into the driver's seat. "Yes. This is Hazel. She gets front-seat privileges."

"But you don't even let *me* sit in front." Jessie huffed and sat back against the seat. Hazel turned three times and settled down into a little wolf ball, looking very smug. "She's spoiled."

"She is not." Wes's jaw tightened and he ran a gentle finger down Hazel's back. "She's an angel. Unlike certain children I could mention."

Jessie found this to be so unfair that she actually kept quiet for the rest of the drive, her voice choked by the injustice of it all. Every once in a while, Hazel would look back at her, those big brown eyes full of entitlement. *An angel*. Jessie snorted and shook her head. More like a furry little demon.

They pulled up to Wes's house.

"We're walking her from here?" Jessie asked, surprised.

"No, I'm petsitting her. I'll walk her around later." He put the car in park and turned off the ignition.

"You mean she's staying here? With you?"

"Yeah. Her person is going out of town."

"Do you do a lot of petsitting? Can I petsit, too?" Jessie asked eagerly. Maybe not this dog, but a nice dog. A dog like Sweetpea.

"One, I only petsit Hazel, and two, absolutely not."

Darn. Jessie scowled at Hazel, who merely lifted her little white snout into the air. So entitled. "Why this one?" Jessie asked. "What's so special about her?"

Wes hesitated. "She was my first client. Her owner was the one who convinced me to start dog walking."

"She did? Why?"

"She travels a lot for work and needed someone to watch Hazel, and I was in a transitional period." He opened his door. "Same time tomorrow, eh, kid?"

"Yeah, I suppose," Jessie grumbled. She had a million more questions, like what exactly a *transitional period* even meant, but she knew Wes was reaching his answering limit. Still, she had to know, "Are you ever going to tell me the other Rules of the Ruff?"

"Eventually."

"When?"

"When you're ready. You need to learn them one at a time, really learn them, or they won't help you. Now get out of my car."

Jessie got out and kicked the door shut behind her. She'd just spent her whole day helping Wes, acting like a human pooper-scooper, and here he was treating her like she was some stupid little kid. She felt like a storm cloud, roiling and angry and dark.

Wes took in her crossed arms and jutting chin. "You spend one morning dog walking and you think you're an expert, is that it?"

"What's the second Rule, Wes?" Jessie demanded.

"Don't be impertinent."

"That's a strange Ruff Rule."

Wes slowly got out of the car and whistled for Hazel. She hopped out and sat down next to him. "The second Rule," he said quietly, "is to be aware of your surroundings." He shut the door and looked Jessie up and down, his eyes narrowed. "Can you tell me where we walked today?"

"The park."

"What dogs did you see there? Which trails did we take?"

Jessie's heart sank. She *didn't* know. She hadn't really been paying attention to those things. "Uh . . ."

"See? You aren't ready."

"I might have been, if you'd told me the Rule earlier."

"But then would you have been practicing your calm and confident energy? Or would you have been too distracted, trying to study everything else?"

Jessie wasn't sure how to answer that.

"That's what I thought," Wes said. "Now scram, kid. I'm tired of your company."

The insult felt like a knife to her gut. "Fine. I'm tired of yours, too!" She stomped off, waiting for him to call her back, to apologize the way adults usually did, but he didn't. He just went inside and shut his door.

Jessie spun, staring at that door. Definitely closed. She turned and headed home. She didn't care if he thought she was irritating. She didn't care if he didn't tell her she did a good job. Didn't care if he told her to go away. She sniffed and swiped angrily at her eyes. It didn't bother her, not one bit.

"Jessie?"

Jessie whipped around. Her heart stuttered, and she took a step back. Max stood a few feet away, wearing that same faded baseball cap over his unruly curls, her soccer ball tucked under one arm.

CHAPTER 5

J essie was painfully aware of every fiber of dog fur that clung to her, of all the sweat and the dirt and the fact that she'd been picking up poop for the past few hours. She wiped her sweaty hands on the back of her pants and tried to ignore the burning in her face. "H-hey, Max."

Max raised his eyebrows. "What have you been doing today? You look a little . . . er . . ."

"A little what?" Jessie crossed her arms over her chest, anger pushing away her embarrassment. "Dirty? Tired? Boyish?"

Now it was his turn to flush. "I'm really sorry about that. I wasn't sure, when I first met you, but then you were so good at soccer . . ."

"Oh, so since I was *good* you thought I *had* to be a boy, is that it?"

Max took a step back. "Yes. I mean, no! Of course not. I mean, er." He coughed a little, then held out her soccer ball in both hands. "Peace offering?"

Jessie scowled, but she took her ball back.

His lips curved up.

"Stop smiling. You're not forgiven."

"Fair enough. How about we play for it, then? If I beat you, we forget about the stupid things I said to you, and we start over?"

"I don't know. That's a lot of stupid on the line for one game to fix."

"Best of three, then?" His grin was back in full force, that foxy smile working its magic. Jessie felt her resolve melting. Not because she cared, really. She just wanted someone to play soccer with.

"Well . . ." she hesitated.

"I mean, unless you're scared. You did lose last time, after all."

That did it. Jessie forgot about how tired she was, forgot her hunger, forgot she'd snuck out that morning and her aunt was probably furious. "Fine. Let's do this." She turned and marched to the park, ignoring Max the whole way.

Three games later, Jessie was forced to concede. She'd won the first game, anger fueling her, but Max had quickly beaten her in the second. That was when she'd started to feel that wild sprint with Angel, her legs getting heavy and slow. She managed to suck it up for the third game, which drew out for almost an hour, but in the end, Max scored the final goal.

Jessie wiped her sweaty hair back from her head and

put her hands on her knees, the world swimming around her. It was so hot she could hear buzzing, and she wasn't sure if it was insects or the air itself.

"Hey there, the name's Max."

"I know who you are." Jessie straightened.

"We're starting over, right?" He grinned, his hand still extended. Jessie scowled at it, but then, reluctantly, she shook it.

"Jessie. Of the female variety," she added.

"Oh, I know." He waggled his eyebrows at her in a way that made her laugh and blush, and she snatched her hand back. Her fingers tingled, and she made a point of wiping her hand on her shirt.

"Ouch," Max said.

"Well, your hand's all sweaty." Jessie shrugged. "Anyhow, I'd better go."

"Cool. See you tomorrow, then?"

"It's a fairly strong possibility."

"Well. I'm not quite sure how to take that, so in my head, you just said yes." He saluted, then headed out of the park.

Jessie found herself smiling as she walked in the opposite direction back to her cousin's house, her ball tucked securely under her arm. Today hadn't turned out so bad, after all. But then her aunt Beatrice opened the door, a blast of cold air churning out around her. Jessie shivered, and not because of the air-conditioning.

Aunt Beatrice's face was all sharp slashes, from the thin white line of her mouth to the narrow slits of her eyes.

Jessie swallowed. "H-hi Aunt Bea."

Aunt Beatrice wasted no time in lecturing her, words like "sneaking out in the early hours of the morning," and "doing whatever you want," and "inconsiderate," and "my responsibility," tumbling from her lips. Jessie imagined herself as a well, letting the words splash inside her, falling to the bottom, the water on top as calm as ever once the ripples faded. It was a pretty image. Calm and confident. Confident and calm.

Aunt Beatrice stopped abruptly. "And now you're smiling. Here I've been worried sick, and you're standing there and smiling in my face."

"I'm not," Jessie said quickly, the first Rule of the Ruff vanishing like dog fur in the wind. "I'm not happy at all, I promise."

Aunt Beatrice rubbed her temples, looking a little like Wes, all worn around the edges.

"Look, it's not like she was out robbing houses or something," Uncle David soothed, coming up behind her.

Aunt Beatrice frowned. "Don't give her ideas, David. This reckless behavior, running around, and look at her! All dirty and grimy and, and . . ."

"Sweaty?" Jessie offered. It was the wrong thing to do. She should have kept her mouth shut.

Aunt Beatrice's nostrils flared, once, twice, the way they did when she was really, truly angry. And ten minutes later, Jessie found herself scrubbing dishes. By hand. It was barbaric.

Her stomach grumbled, but apparently she'd missed lunch, and she didn't have the nerve to ask about food. She wasn't that brave.

The rest of Jessie's afternoon trudged by in a brutal flurry of housework. She did it without complaint, trying to turn it into a competition. How many dishes could she wash in one minute? (Seven.) How fast could she vacuum the living room? (Three and a half minutes, not counting the corners, which her aunt made her do over.) Could she dust as well with her left hand as with her right? (Not really.)

"Your dad's on the phone," Uncle David said, jolting Jessie away from the stack of books she was dusting.

"Really?" Jessie leapt to her feet, the books tumbling to the floor in one big jumble.

He winced.

"Oh. Sorry." She bent to pick them up.

"I'll get them. Just go answer the phone. Also," Uncle David glanced around, then produced a peanut butter and jelly sandwich, "here. Dinner's soon, but I figured you'd be hun—"

Jessie snatched the sandwich, stuffing half of it into her mouth in one bite.

"—gry," Uncle David finished, his eyes widening.

"Tanks," Jessie said around a mouthful of sandwich. She hurried into the kitchen, where her aunt and uncle still had one of those old-fashioned phones, the kind where the phone was connected by a curly wire. Her dad had said she could get a cell phone when she was in high school, but for now she was reduced to this.

Jessie chewed, chewed, swallowed, then picked the phone up off the kitchen table. "Hello?"

"Hey there." Her dad's warm voice filled her ear.

Jessie pressed the phone against her head, relief flooding her, along with a strong pang of homesickness. She missed her dad. She told him so, the words flooding out of her, and suddenly she was talking about Wes and the Rules of the Ruff. She left out the bit about Aunt Beatrice being angry and all the unnecessary housework. Her dad had the bad habit of sympathizing with his sister, and she didn't want to get into an argument.

"And he let the Klee Kai sit in front, can you believe it?" she finished.

"Klee Kai?" Her dad said the words awkwardly.

"It's basically a mini husky."

"Well that sounds about the cutest dog ever."

Jessie sighed. "I suppose."

"So . . . you still want a dog of your own?"

The breath caught in Jessie's throat.

"Hello? Jessie?"

"Y-yes, of course I still do. Why?" Her heart slammed into her chest as she waited, the silence on the other end lasting a beat, two beats, three.

"We-ell," her dad drawled out the word, the way he always did when he was about to unveil something. "They've decided to hire me on permanently after the summer—"

"They have?"

"Oh yes. I'll have a steady, full-time job, no more moving around. Good pay, too. So, maybe that means it's time to really put down some roots. And what better way than with a family dog? Your mom—" He stopped, and Jessie felt her heart stop, too. Her mom had been dead for four years, and Jessie could count the times her dad had talked about her since on one hand. It was as if her death had ripped a hole in their lives that no words could ever fill, and so he didn't even try. "We always planned to get a family dog," he continued softly. "When we thought you were ready."

Jessie slid her back against the wall until she was sitting on the floor, her fingers curled into the phone wire. "Do you really mean it?" she whispered.

"I'm serious as a heart attack," her dad said, his voice extra boisterous, and Jessie pretended not to hear the quaver beneath it. "Now, you be good for your aunt and uncle, and keep learning from this Wes fellow, and we'll have ourselves a deal. Yeah?"

"Yeah."

"OK, kiddo, I gotta run. Love you!"

"Love you, too." Jessie sat there long after her father had hung up. Her ear was filled with the buzzing of the dead phone line, but her head was too full to notice. A dog, a dog of her very own.

When you're a little older, we'll get a dog . . . Her mother's hands brushing through her hair, twisting it into braids, the smell of her lotion filling Jessie's bedroom, coconut and vanilla.

What's a little older? Jessie had asked. She liked having a concrete goal to aim for.

Jessie remembered her mother laughing at that, but now she couldn't remember what her laugh had sounded like, couldn't remember the exact way she smiled or the precise tone of her voice when she'd answered: *When you're ready, honey. When you're ready.*

Jessie closed her eyes, letting the memory fade around her. Her heart ached the way it always did when she thought of her mother. Words could never fill the hole her absence had created, but maybe a dog could.

CHAPTER 6

T he next morning, Jessie woke before her alarm even went off. She got dressed quickly in the darkness of the room, choosing a pair of long shorts and a T-shirt by feel.

"Mom's going to kill you if you keep sneaking out," Ann said.

Jessie jumped.

Ann's face was a light blur in the shadows. "You have to be back in time for lunch, OK? I can probably cover for you until then."

"Th-thanks," Jessie said, surprised. Ann almost sounded like the old Ann.

"Don't mention it." Ann flopped back down on her pillow, and once again she was Ann-*Marie*. "I mean seriously, don't mention it."

Jessie snuck into the kitchen and grabbed a banana. She hesitated, grabbed a second one, and then quietly left the house. As she jogged toward Wes's house, she replayed yesterday's phone conversation in her head. A dog. She was getting a dog. But what kind should she choose?

She pictured Angel, with those big brown eyes. Maybe a pit bull. But then she remembered how strong Angel was. Did she really want to walk someone like that every morning? Well, it would get her in good shape, that was for sure.

Or maybe a Lab, like Sweetpea or Lady. Or an Australian shepherd, like Presto. Or . . . or a hairy muppet-like dog, like Zelda, the wire-haired griffon she'd met yesterday in Wes's first pack. She was super sweet and energetic, and she had the same bushy eyebrows as Wes. For a moment, Jessie pictured Wes's usual scowl on that canine face and smiled.

"Someone looks happy this morning," Wes remarked as he sipped his tea on his front porch. "Awfully happy indeed for someone who's going to spend the morning picking up dog poo." He grinned. "And look at that, now I'm happy, too."

Jessie sighed, letting the images of her future dog fade around her. "Let's get this over with, then."

"That's the spirit." He put his mug down on that same ceramic coaster as before. Jessie wondered if he just always left that out here. Such a strange man. She tried not to let it bother her, the lonely mug on the lonely coaster, as she trailed him to his car.

True to his word, Wes had Jessie follow along cleaning up after the dogs again. He did not let her walk any of them, although she got to leash and unleash each and every one. She met most of her old friends from yesterday, except, "No Sweetpea?" she asked as they drove past the Lab's house.

Wes shook his head. "Owners called this morning. They don't need any more walks this week." His jaw tightened. "Always hate when that happens. Throws off the balance."

Other than that, the morning went about the same as the day before, only this time, Jessie was careful to keep track of their surroundings, their routes, the addresses for the dogs, and the other dogs they passed. Wes also gave her tips as she trailed along behind him and his pack. "See how they're organized?" he said. "Keep each dog in place and don't let the leashes cross."

"Is that a Rule of the Ruff?" Jessie asked.

"No, it's just good common sense."

Jessie frowned. At this rate, it was going to take forever to learn all the Rules. Still, she had to admit it was impressive, the way the dogs walked so calmly for him, with two on one side, three on the other. Wes's arms were relaxed, the leashes loose in his hands at his sides, their ends clipped securely into the hip pack he always wore on the job. Calm and confident. She tried imitating his rolling stride, the way he kept his knees slightly bent. It reminded her of a sailor crossing a stormy deck, anchored by dogs.

Wes glanced at her. "What," he said slowly, "are you doing?"

"I'm walking like you," Jessie said.

"I really hope I don't look like that."

Jessie kept at it anyhow, but it was hard work, and by the time Wes let her stop for the morning, she was exhausted.

"Want to quiz me?" she asked as he pulled into his driveway. She could see Hazel's little face peeking out from the window of his house.

"On?" he asked.

"On our surroundings today."

"Not really."

"Oh," Jessie said, disappointed. "Well, I can tell you where we went, where each of the dogs lives, and—"

"I'm going to stop you there, kid." Wes got out of the car and opened his front door, whistling for Hazel. She tore out of the house, howling her little husky howl and prancing around him.

"Will you at least tell me the third Rule?"

Wes narrowed his eyes. "You're not ready for the third Rule."

Jessie opened her mouth to argue, but Wes held up his hand. "This is not a discussion. You're not ready. But," he said slowly, reluctantly, "you did well today, kid."

Jessie blinked, his words washing over her in a rush of warmth. Wes wasn't like other adults; he wouldn't pat you on the head and tell you "good effort" just for trying. Which meant she'd really earned this praise. She *had* done well. It felt like she'd won something, and she couldn't stop the grin from spreading wide across her face.

Hazel trotted over and licked her on the leg.

"Even Hazel thinks so, and she's a tough critic," he added.

"Thanks, girl." Jessie crouched down and ran a finger

along Hazel's soft little head. The dog's curly tail wagged once, twice, and then she trotted over to Wes. As Jessie left them behind, she felt like she was floating, her feet finally gliding like Wes's did along the sidewalk.

She swung by her cousin's house in plenty of time for lunch, which was always an informal affair. "Catch as catch can," as her aunt said. Jessie made herself a sandwich and ate it quickly, wondering if Max would be at the park again by now. She hesitated, then went searching for Uncle David. She figured it would be better to ask permission before leaving again, just in case, and her uncle was definitely the best choice.

Jessie could hear Aunt Beatrice talking quietly on the phone in her bedroom. She tiptoed past and found Uncle David in his home office, playing some silly game on his computer.

"What's up, Jessie?" Uncle David leaned back in his chair, the legs creaking.

"Is it OK if I go to the park this afternoon?"

"Sure, sure."

"Aunt Beatrice won't mind?"

"Nah. Go have fun." He waved her off, already turning back to his computer. Jessie smiled triumphantly as she snuck back into the kitchen and made herself another sandwich.

"How much do you eat?" Ann asked from her perch at the table.

"As much as I need." Jessie took a large bite. "No Loralee today?" she mumbled around her food.

"That's disgusting." Ann flipped another page in her

magazine. "And she said she had some sort of errand to run. She'll come by later."

Jessie mentally resolved to be far away whenever "later" happened to be. She chewed another large bite of sandwich, scrutinizing her cousin's face, noticing the mascara, the eyeliner, the way she styled her bangs. Ann looked nothing like the frizzy-headed girl she'd been at the start of last summer.

"Done staring at me yet?" Ann scowled.

Jessie quickly dropped her gaze, her chest filling with that same humiliated feeling only Ann and Loralee seemed to inspire. Finishing her sandwich, she left the house without another word, stopping only to grab her soccer ball from under the porch.

Max grinned at her from their usual meeting spot under the third elm tree. Usual spot. Jessie rolled that around in her mind. She and Max had a usual spot. For some reason, it made her stomach clench and her skin tingle, and she had trouble meeting Max's eyes as she jogged over. Instead she kept her gaze on the ball. "Ready to play?" she asked.

"Uh, good morning? Nice to see you? Hello, even?"

Jessie looked up, forcing herself to hold his gaze. His fox smile was in full force. She took a deep breath, let it out. "It's actually afternoon."

"Oh."

"And I don't have time for small talk. I'm busy focusing on my upcoming win."

"Ah. Your 'win.'" He wiggled his fingers like quotation

marks next to his head. "I think you're in for a real disappointment."

"Your face is a disappointment," Jessie said, and just like that, the weird feeling left her, the tension gone.

"Well, I guess it's on, then." Max's brown eyes shone as he lunged and slapped the ball out of her hands.

They'd been playing for about twenty minutes when a voice trilled, "Max! Oh, Max!"

Max turned to look. Jessie didn't even hesitate, just ran past him and kicked the ball into his goal. "Ha!"

"Hey! That's hardly fair."

"You've gotta stay focused on the game. All's fair in soccer and . . ." Her eyes slid past him, and she finally noticed the girl leaning against a tree. A girl with long chestnut-brown hair and overly glossed lips. ". . . war," she finished.

"I was hoping I'd catch you here." Loralee pushed away from the tree and sauntered over. She was wearing a pair of skin-tight black capris with silver swirls around the hems and a snug white athletic top. Definitely not her usual look, and it gave Jessie a bad feeling, like she'd just bitten into an apple and found half a worm.

"I'm up two. Game point," Jessie said, doing her best to ignore Loralee.

"Are you losing?" Loralee's lips curled in a small flirty smile. "To Jessie? To a *girl*?" Her wide brown eyes flicked past Max, fixing on Jessie for the first time. Jessie straightened and met that gaze head on. She recognized the look: She was being challenged. "Maybe you need another girl to show you how it's done."

"You want to play? Against *me?*" Jessie asked.

Loralee shrugged, a slow, deliberate gesture that pulled her shirt up a bit, exposing her stomach. "Or I could play against Max," she purred.

"Er," Max said.

"Max and I are in the middle of a game," Jessie argued. "Right, Max?"

"Er," Max said again. He kept looking at Loralee, but sideways, as if he didn't want her to know he was looking. *He shouldn't bother trying to hide it,* Jessie thought bitterly. He was doing a terrible job. So obvious.

"Hey." Jessie tossed the soccer ball right at his face. He blinked, catching it an inch in front of his nose. "We still doing this, or what?"

He grinned, his teeth dimpling his bottom lip. "Oh, we're doing this." He glanced once more at Loralee. "Sorry, uh, Laura."

"Loralee." She snapped the name without its usual drawn-out lilt.

Max rubbed the back of his neck. "Loralee. Well, we're in the middle of a game already. Maybe later?"

"Maybe . . . later?" Loralee repeated slowly, like she just couldn't believe it.

"Yeah, later." Max was already turning away from her.

Jessie pictured herself as a soccer ball soaring effortlessly into a goal, right past the goalie's out-stretched arms, the net wrapping her in its embrace. Out of the corner of her eye, she saw Loralee watching them, her eyes narrowed, her face an ugly mask. It made Jessie feel triumphant. It also made her nervous.

Max kicked the ball and Jessie had to sprint to catch up. When she looked up again, Loralee was gone, but for the rest of the game, Jessie's skin prickled like someone was standing right behind her.

"Can't seem too eager," Max confided when the game was up.

"What?" Jessie wiped her sweaty brow on her sleeve.

"With girls. You know." He hesitated. "Or I guess maybe you don't."

Jessie sniffed. "I know all about girls. I mean, I *am* one. Remember?"

"I thought we were starting over?"

"We are."

"Doesn't that mean you have to forget about earlier mistakes?"

"Nope," Jessie declared. "It just means I'll keep playing you in soccer."

Max chuckled. "You are a character, Jessie. A real character." He brushed grass from his shorts. "See you tomorrow?"

"Stranger things have happened."

"That's what I thought." He gave her a mock salute and sauntered off across the park. Jessie found herself watching him walk, the way his sweaty T-shirt clung to his shoulder blades.

CHAPTER 7

Jessie managed to slip into the house without her aunt noticing, and she used the opportunity to take a quick shower and change. That ought to keep Aunt Bea happy. Or, at least, less unhappy. She even ran her fingers through her hair, which was basically the same as brushing it, then headed into the kitchen, where her aunt was busy chopping vegetables. "Can I help set the table?" Jessie asked.

Aunt Beatrice paused, knife lifted. She eyed Jessie suspiciously. "What did you do? Did you break something?"

"No, no, just trying to be helpful." Jessie grinned. She figured if her dad was going to get her a dog, she could stand to be a little nicer to her aunt. Plus, the sooner the table was set, the sooner they'd eat. "Really, Aunt Bea, I didn't break anything. You can put the knife down."

That actually brought a small smile to her aunt's lips, and a few minutes later, the table in the dining room was set.

"Ann's not back yet, so we'll have to wait," Aunt Beatrice said as Uncle David sat down at the table.

Jessie groaned and flopped down in her customary place in the far corner, the wall at her back. Her stomach grumbled. She imagined it as a pack of dogs, all sitting in the back of the car, ready to walk.

"Stop being dramatic, Jessie," her aunt said.

"I wasn't being dramatic. *This* is 'being dramatic.'" Jessie put the back of her hand against her forehead and swooned against the wall.

Uncle David chuckled, but Aunt Beatrice just shook her head and swept out to the kitchen, returning with a large platter of food.

It was Thursday, which meant it was fish day. Sure as clockwork. Jessie wasn't a big fan of fish, especially the way her aunt cooked it. It always tasted dry, like she was eating a salty sweater. But it was better than nothing, and she'd learned long ago that complaining about the menu meant going to bed without any food at all. At least they'd have a side of rice pilaf, which she usually liked, as long as her aunt didn't add onions to it.

"Maybe we should just start," Uncle David suggested. "It seems like some people here are getting a little hangry."

"'Hangry'?" Jessie raised her eyebrows.

"Angry when hungry," her uncle explained. "It's what all the kids are saying these days." Her uncle was a fifth-grade math teacher. He liked to think that made him cool.

"My father would cry to hear you butchering the English language like that," Jessie said. Her father had never gotten his college degree; Jessie was pretty sure her unexpected arrival had stopped his education plans. She'd heard her aunt whispering about it a couple of times in the past. But he read a lot, more than anyone she'd ever known, and was a stickler for proper speech.

"Anyways," Uncle David picked up one of the serving spoons, "Ann can just join when—"

"Sorry I'm late!" Ann bounced into the room. "Uh, is it OK if Loralee joins us?"

Jessie's heart sank down to her feet. No, lower than that. She felt like it had left her body entirely and been replaced with a rock.

Loralee's eyes met Jessie's and she smiled her little smile, her lips curving just the slightest bit. And just like that, Jessie was no longer hungry.

"Only if it's not inconvenient," Loralee purred, gaze still on Jessie. "I'd hate to be a nuisance."

"There's not enough fish," Jessie pointed out. "There are only four pieces."

"Jessie!" Aunt Beatrice smiled at Loralee. "Of course you can join us. Ann, grab your friend a chair and place setting, would you? And I'll just do . . . this." She used a knife to cut the largest piece of fish into two smaller pieces. "There. All fixed."

And, of course, Jessie was given one of the fish halves. The smaller of the halves, more like a third really. She looked at it sadly. The other part of the fish was dropped onto Ann's plate, and Loralee, the intruder, got a whole piece to herself. Not that she'd even eat it. She usually just nibbled at her food, just enough so no one else could have it. Then she'd claim to be "oh so full."

Jessie stabbed into her fish viciously, picturing it as

Loralee's face, and had a momentary feeling of satisfaction as it flaked apart.

"Has Jessie told you about her new boyfriend yet?" Loralee asked.

Uncle David choked on his bite of fish, Aunt Beatrice gasped, and Ann looked down at her plate, her face reddening.

"B-boyfriend?" Jessie managed, her feeling of satisfaction drying up faster than Aunt Bea's cooking. "I don't have—" Max's face swam through her mind, and suddenly she was redder than Ann. Was that who Loralee meant?

"What is she talking about, Jessie?" Aunt Beatrice asked.

"I-I don't know. I don't have a boyfriend."

"Bea, this is Jessie we're talking about," Uncle David said.

Even though he was defending her, his comment made Jessie feel even worse.

"I know, it's so surprising." Loralee's smile was as sharp and vicious as the knife she sliced into her fish. She took a tiny, tiny bite.

"Is this why you've been sneaking off in the mornings?" Aunt Beatrice asked.

Jessie spared a glance for her cousin, who wouldn't meet her eyes. So much for covering for her. "No, Aunt Beatrice," she said. "I've been meeting a boy in the park, but only in the afternoon for soccer. That's it, just soccer."

Aunt Beatrice's nostrils flared, and Jessie braced herself. "Then where have you been going in the morning?"

Jessie hesitated, but she'd already told her dad. Her

aunt would hear about it from him anyhow. So, reluctantly, she told them about walking dogs with Wes.

"You mean old Wes?" Uncle David asked, surprised. "Wes the Dog Man? Blond hair, scruffy face, talks kind of funny?"

"That sounds like him," Jessie said.

"You should stay away from him. He's not very friendly," Aunt Beatrice said.

"Yeah, doesn't like kids," Uncle David chimed in.

"Wasn't he the one whose wife ran off?" Ann asked.

"Ann-Marie," her mother said warningly.

"What? I heard she took the dog and everything."

"Stop spreading rumors." Aunt Beatrice turned toward Jessie and put on her "I'm your friendly aunt" smile. It looked painful. "Jessie, I know how you feel about dogs, but I think you should leave Wes alone. He's been through a lot," she glared at Ann, who sat up straighter in her chair, "and I don't want you to bother him."

"Isn't your new friend a dog walker?" Uncle David asked, nudging his wife. "Maybe she'd take Jessie on."

"No," Jessie said quickly. She didn't want to work for another dog walker. Wes was rude, and kind of strange, and . . . well, unpleasant all around, actually. But despite his grumpiness, she knew she was winning him over. *You did well today, kid.* He'd admitted that, just this morning. If she left him now, she'd be letting him down.

"Jessie—" Aunt Beatrice began.

"Wes already said I could work for him," Jessie said. "And I told my dad, and he's fine with it." She ate the last of her fish, ignoring the pointed look her aunt gave her uncle. Jessie didn't want to disappoint Wes, and besides, she only knew two Rules of the Ruff; she had to learn the rest of them. It felt like a challenge, and she didn't like to back down from a challenge. Would a dog back down?

"If James is OK with it." Uncle David shrugged.

"James doesn't always have the best judgment. And he's not here right now, not responsible for the safety of this child."

"Wes is safe enough. Besides, it keeps Jessie busy."

Aunt Beatrice hesitated, but Jessie could see how this argument appealed to her. Last summer, once Ann had stopped hanging out with her, Jessie had been a little . . . destructive. She hadn't meant to be, but she'd been bored, and sad, and, OK, kind of angry. "Fine," Aunt Beatrice said. "But only if you're not bothering that poor man."

Uncle David winked at Jessie, and she relaxed against her seat. She could keep working for Wes, and there was no more embarrassing talk of boyfriends over dinner. For the second time that day, she felt like she'd beaten Loralee.

Loralee set down her fork and knife with a soft *plink*.

"Aren't you hungry, Loralee?" Aunt Bea asked.

With her eyes on Jessie, Loralee shook her head. "No, thanks Beatrice, I'm oh so full now." She smiled her glossy cat smile, and Jessie knew Loralee wasn't beaten at all. No, she was just biding her time, waiting for the next moment to pounce.

CHAPTER 8

Jessie trudged back through the park, her soccer ball tucked under one arm. She'd just spent yet another morning on poop-scooping duty, and still Wes had refused to tell her the third Rule. How was she supposed to master the Rules of the Ruff if she didn't even know what they were? Still, she felt like she'd really perfected the art of leashing dogs and dropping them back off at their homes. Her record from the car to the house and back was now twenty-four seconds, and even Wes had seemed impressed with her efficiency. It had been enough to make her feel a little proud, despite her role as human pooper-scooper.

That is, until Max hadn't bothered to show up at the park afterward. And the worst part was Jessie had actually waited for him.

She stopped at one of the water fountains along the elm-lined path for a quick drink. Covertly she glanced back across the park in case Max was just running late. Really late.

A flash of pink caught her eye. Straightening, Jessie

stared across the park at a familiar-looking harness. It was on wrong, the leash clipped to a loop in back instead of attached to the front, so the Labrador wearing it was able to pull to her heart's content. A Labrador who looked suspiciously like . . . "Sweetpea?" Jessie whispered. And walking her . . . that same woman from before, her black hair in long perfect braids, her arms straight and stiff as she let Sweetpea yank her around like some kind of amateur.

Jessie remembered Wes's words from yesterday: *Her owners called this morning. They don't need any more walks this week.*

What was happening? What did this mean? Frowning, she made up her mind and headed back to Wes's house.

"You're sure?" Wes sat on the porch, Hazel curled up on a pillow next to him. A pillow. Not even a dog bed but an actual fluffy, down feather–stuffed pillow.

"Definitely. Same dog, same woman," Jessie said. "And is that your pillow she's sleeping on? Or does she get her own personal pillow?" Jessie wasn't sure which would be worse.

Hazel lifted her little snout and yawned, her tongue pink against the dark fur of her face. She licked her chops, shifted once, and settled more comfortably. She really was kind of cute . . . Jessie shook herself. She wasn't going to fall for that. "Wes?" she asked, realizing he'd been silent.

Wes ran a finger down the groove between his eyebrows. Then he stood abruptly.

Jessie scrambled to her feet, too. "What's the plan?"

"Plan?"

"She's stealing your dog walks, isn't she?" It was the only thing that made sense. "We have to stop her."

Wes scowled. "Let's not jump to conclusions. I need to think this over first."

"But—"

"Go away, irritating child. I can't think with you jabbering at me." He went inside and slammed the door.

Jessie stared at the closed door. She shouldn't be surprised. She shouldn't. But when it opened a few seconds later, something inside her relaxed. "I knew you'd—"

Wes whistled for Hazel, then slammed the door shut again behind her, leaving Jessie alone on the porch.

Jessie's shoulders slumped. She trudged down Wes's steps, hesitating at the bottom. If she went home right now, she'd just sit around feeling miserable. Might as well check one last time for Max.

She headed to the park, her heart lifting as she spotted a very familiar blue hat up ahead. She sped up, then stopped dead as she realized: Max wasn't waiting at the park for *her*. No, he was already busy playing soccer with someone else. A slim girl, her long brown hair pulled back in a low ponytail that slithered and slipped around her shoulders as she ran.

Loralee. Max was playing soccer . . . with Loralee.

Jessie slunk behind an elm. She couldn't tear her eyes away from them, from Max laughing, laughing with Loralee. Her lips were even curled in a smile, a real one, as she kicked the soccer ball.

Jessie's throat hurt. It felt worse than sprinting with Angel. She squeezed her eyes shut, then opened them again, watching as Max dribbled the ball past Loralee. Loralee darted in, snaking the ball from between his feet. He was definitely going easy on her, but she was actually pretty good, too. Who'd have thought?

"Max!" a woman called, and Max turned.

It was the other dog walker, waving from across the park.

Jessie shrank against the tree, her mouth falling open. How did *that woman* know *Max?* Wait a second . . . Jessie squinted at the dog next to the woman. Zelda. She had taken Zelda; Jessie would recognize those bushy eyebrows anywhere. It was like getting hit in the face with a soccer ball. Dimly she observed that Zelda's leash wasn't even clipped in to the woman's hip pack. Probably for the best, since her pack looked flimsy enough that one good tug would likely snap it.

"Who's that?" Loralee eyed the other woman.

"Oh, just my mom." Max raised a hand half-heartedly.

His mom?

The world stopped moving for a second, two seconds, then sped up so fast it was like Jessie was going to spin right off it. His mom. The dog-walk thief was Max's mom.

Loralee darted in suddenly, stealing the ball from Max and sprinting toward the goal.

"You are such a cheat!" Max grabbed her arm and pulled her around. She grinned up at him, their bodies still touching, before she whispered something that made him blush and let her go. As she jogged away from him, laughing, she glanced at the line of elm trees, her eyes meeting Jessie's.

Loralee smirked, her steps slowing.

Jessie pushed herself off the tree, turned, and ran, not waiting to see if Loralee would say anything, not wanting Max to know she'd been there.

CHAPTER 9

Jessie raced inside the house.

"Jessie, what's—" Ann began.

Slam!

Jessie shut herself inside the bathroom.

"Are you crying?"

"No!" Jessie yelled. "Just, just leave me alone." She turned on the shower, letting the noise of the water block out everything else. Then she sat on the floor, wrapped her arms around her legs, and buried her face in her knees.

She didn't care about stupid Max playing soccer with someone else. She didn't even care that he'd obviously waited so he wouldn't run into her there, that he'd obviously planned on playing with someone else without telling her. If it had been anyone else, anyone at all . . . but no. It had to be *Loralee.*

Loralee, with her glossy lips and her mocking tone and her ability to make Jessie feel like she was smaller and more pathetic than anyone. Loralee, who took everything from her. Loralee.

Jessie could still remember the moment she'd met the older girl. It was burned into her memory, humiliation holding it firmly in place no matter how hard she tried burying it.

It had been midway through last summer.

Jessie was wearing one of her dad's overlarge T-shirts with a piece of rope tied around her waist so it looked like a robe. She and Ann were pretending to be wizards out in the front yard. Ann grumbled that they were getting a little old for games of make-believe, but Jessie could still get her cousin to play most of the time, even if she refused to dress up. At least she'd still wear the hat.

"OK, Ann, it's your turn to make the life elixir," she said.

Ann sighed. "Are you seriously dying already? I thought we just made some."

"I'm all out." Jessie held out her mug and tipped it over, showing how empty it was. She grinned at her cousin.

"Your tongue is blue," Ann laughed.

"I told you! I'm dying. Wizard duels are no joke."

"Fine, fine. Here, give me your cup."

"Goblet," Jessie corrected.

"Goblet. I'll be right back." Ann slipped inside the house, the top of her pointed homemade wizard hat brushing the doorframe.

"Oh. My. God."

Jessie looked around.

A girl was staring at her from the sidewalk on the

other side of Aunt Bea's rose bushes. She was tall and slender and, there was no other word for it, *glossy*. Her lips shimmered, her sequined purple tank top glimmered, and her long brown hair shone like polished wood in the sun. "What are you *wearing?*" she demanded.

At eleven, Jessie had been full of confidence, but in the face of so much scorn coming from someone so pretty, she felt herself wavering. "A, uh, wizard's robe," she half-mumbled.

"A wizard's robe. Really."

Jessie shrugged. "It could be." She could feel her face burning, but she didn't care what some stranger thought. Did she?

"OK, Jess—" Ann stopped abruptly in the doorway. In the blink of an eye she'd shoved her pointed hat off her head and smoothed her hair. "L-Loralee?" She stepped outside, gaping at the stranger.

"Oh. Hey. You were in my math class this year, right?" Loralee said.

"Um, yeah," Ann managed. "I sat behind you. I was also in your English, and Social Studies, and—"

"Fine, fine." Loralee tossed her head like she was shaking off a fly. "Anyhow, I'm stuck here for the summer, and it is so boring. Everyone else is out of town vacationing or at camp or whatever." She looked Ann up and down, her eyes narrowing critically. "It's Ann-Marie, right?"

"Uh, sure."

"You want to come walk with me? That is, unless you're busy." She flicked a glance at Jessie.

"No. No, I'm not busy." Now it was Ann's turn to look at Jessie. "This is just my cousin."

Just my cousin. It was worse than a slap; it was like a punch to the rib cage. Jessie felt like she had no air and no voice.

Ann dropped Jessie's mug on the picnic table before following Loralee. Blue Kool-Aid sloshed out the side, staining the table in a ring. Jessie stared at that stain as her cousin left her behind, without a glance, without a thought. As if Jessie was nothing but a stain, too.

And when the two girls were out of sight, Jessie shoved the mug off the table, where it shattered on the cement beneath it.

Jessie breathed in the steam filling the small bathroom.

"Stop wasting water!" Aunt Beatrice pounded on the door. "Jessie? You hear me?"

Jessie's memories scattered like squirrels in a dog park. She turned off the water, wiped her face, and left the safety of the bathroom. She could feel her aunt staring at her and knew her face was probably all red and splotchy.

Aunt Beatrice opened her mouth, her face pinched with concern, but then she shook her head and walked away. Like she didn't want to know, didn't want to get involved.

Jessie didn't care, though. She didn't need her aunt's help and didn't *want* her concern. All she needed was to learn the Rules of the Ruff, and she would get her dog at the end of the summer, and then she'd never have to worry about being left behind again.

Max was just a stupid boy; she wouldn't waste any more time on him. And Ann was just another silly pawn.

But Loralee . . .

Loralee had taken Ann. And now she'd taken Max. And Jessie was tired of losing people to her enemy. Her anger glowed hotter as she pictured Loralee's glossy, smug little smile.

Loralee had to pay.

CHAPTER 10

Jessie skipped dinner that night, claiming she wasn't feeling well. She was too angry to eat, her stomach full of rage. Instead, she hid in Ann's bedroom and began a list of ways to get revenge on Loralee. She jotted down a few ideas but quickly ran out. Maybe she could just kick a soccer ball right at her face?

Jessie considered this idea. It definitely had appeal, but she doubted she'd actually do it. Not only was it a blatant misuse of a perfectly good soccer ball, but it seemed a little too brutal. Besides, Max would probably just feel sorry for Loralee and fall madly in love with her once she was all injured and vulnerable. Not that Jessie cared or anything. But still.

She could . . . cut Loralee's hair? Hmm. Maybe.

"Hey, you OK?" Ann asked.

Jessie jumped and dropped her notebook. "Don't—" she began, but it was too late. Ann had already picked it up.

"How to Make Loralee Suffer," she read. "Number one: Steal her lip gloss." Her own lips quirked in a small smile. "You're really not very good at this, are you?"

"Revenge doesn't come easily to me," Jessie muttered, snatching back her notebook. "Are you going to tell Loralee?"

"That you're plotting to steal her lip gloss? Or, what was number two? Sending her anonymous letters about how ugly her clothes are?" Ann shook her head. "I'll let it be a surprise." She flopped onto her bed.

"You're not mad?" Jessie asked, surprised.

"No. I get why you don't like her. I mean, she's really fun, and I think if you got to know her better—"

Jessie made a rude noise.

Ann sighed. "But I understand," she finished quietly. She looked somehow smaller than normal, like she was slowly folding into herself, disappearing into the bed beneath her.

"Are you on the outs with Loralee?" Jessie asked.

"On the outs? No. Why?"

"You're not hanging out as much."

Ann blew her bangs off her forehead. "Well, she's got a new toy to amuse herself with this summer. It's kind of what she does."

"New toy?"

"You know. Max."

"He's not a toy," Jessie snapped.

Ann tilted her head to the side, studying Jessie. "You like him," she realized.

"I do not!"

Ann sat up. "Is it true? The great Jessie Jamison has a crush on a boy?"

"Shut up, Ann. I don't like him. I just, he was fun to play soccer with. That's all."

"And he sure does have a nice smile, yeah? And those legs!" Ann mock swooned.

Jessie threw a pillow at her. "I said shut it, Ann."

"I'm sorry, I'm sorry," Ann giggled. "I'll stop." She was quiet, but only for a minute, before adding, "Loralee usually gets bored pretty quickly. She'll probably drop Max in a week or two anyhow."

Jessie didn't respond, and silence built around them, awkward and uncomfortable as it pushed its way into every corner of the room. Jessie felt it like an avalanche, cold and crushing and full of all the reasons she no longer really liked her cousin. Reasons she had almost forgotten. Almost.

She climbed onto her bed and pulled the covers up around herself. A minute later, Ann flicked off the light.

Jessie lay awake a long time, listening to her cousin breathing. She could tell Ann wasn't asleep yet either, but neither of them said anything as the minutes ticked on. Maybe there wasn't anything else to say.

CHAPTER 11

The next morning Jessie got up and dressed at the first peep from her alarm.

"Seriously, Jessie? It's Saturday," Ann grumbled.

"Do dogs care about the weekend?"

"You are such a weirdo."

Jessie ignored her. She had work to do.

Wes wasn't out on the porch when Jessie got there. Frowning, she knocked at his door. She could hear the distinctive high-pitched howling of Hazel inside. She knocked again.

"*Howoooooooo*," Hazel sang.

"Hey, Hazel-bear, quiet down," Wes said as he opened the door.

"Hazel-bear? Really?" Jessie shook her head.

"What do you want, kid?"

"Same thing I always want. To go walk some dogs!" Jessie grinned and pumped her arms up and down.

"It's Saturday."

"Yeah but—"

"I don't walk dogs on Saturday."

"But Hazel—"

"Special case. I don't *usually* walk dogs on Saturday. Or Sunday, for that matter, so don't bother showing your face here tomorrow, either."

This time Jessie was ready, and she wedged her foot in the way before Wes could shut the door in her face.

"Do you mind?" Wes demanded.

"Actually, I'd prefer if you stopped doing that," Jessie admitted.

"Get off my porch."

"No."

Wes sighed and let the door fall open. "What," he said again, slowly and deliberately, "do you want?"

"I want to talk strategy with you. She's got another one."

"She who? Another what?"

"The enemy! Another dog! I saw her with Zelda yesterday at the park."

"*Howoooo. Howooooooooooo!*"

"Hazel!" Wes barked. "*Shh.*"

"*HOWOOOOO!*"

Across the street, a neighbor pushed back her curtains and glared at them.

Wes shook his head. "Come in."

Jessie hesitated. "R-really?"

"Either that or go home. It's no skin off my back. But I have to check on Hazel before she wakes the whole neighborhood." Wes stepped away from the door, leaving it open. Waiting.

Jessie took a careful step inside, then another one, and looked around.

She wasn't sure what she was expecting, but his house looked normal. Or at least, this part of his house did. There was a small entryway by the front door, with a series of knobs on the left for hanging coats and, in Wes's case, extra leashes and his dog-walking hip pack. To the right was a shoe rack with three pairs of beat-up sneakers, and beside them, a small stack of folded yellow towels balanced on top of a basket. It all looked surprisingly tidy and organized.

Above the shoe rack a sign proclaimed: "Take Your Shoes Off, You Filthy Animal," complete with a sketch of a pig in sneakers.

Jessie took off her shoes, then walked through the entryway into the kitchen. It was small but clean, dominated by an old-fashioned refrigerator in the far corner and a small round table with two chairs in the middle. There was a single magnet on the fridge, a large white circle with the words: "Dogs: Because People Suck" written in cartoonish maroon letters. And underneath the magnet . . . Jessie leaned in, squinting. A man crouched with his arm around a dog. He was smiling, and it took Jessie a few seconds before she realized it was a picture of Wes. A really old picture of Wes. He didn't have that same deep furrow between his eyes and his hair was darker. She reached toward the photo—

"If you're done nosing about," Wes said.

Jessie jumped, knocking the magnet off the fridge.

"S-sorry." She picked up the photo. She realized it was folded; with a glance at Wes's retreating back she flicked the folded side out. A woman with a round, happy face and long, frizzy, blond hair smiled back at her. Now that Jessie was looking at the whole picture, she could see how the woman's shoulder brushed against Wes's, the dog leash wound around her hand.

She remembered what Ann had said the other night, about Wes's wife running off. Was this a picture of her? *I heard she took the dog and everything.*

Feeling uncomfortable, Jessie carefully refolded it so the woman was once again hidden, then used the magnet to stick it back to the fridge. She spared one last look at the image of Wes, young and happy, before hurrying through the kitchen to the living room.

And stopped. There was an entire shelf filled with LEGO sets. Spaceships. Castles. Some kind of fancy building with a domed top. "Whoa," Jessie breathed, reaching out to touch them.

"Don't even think about it," Wes said. He was watching her with narrowed eyes from a large reclining chair, Hazel on his lap.

Jessie sighed and dropped her hand. She wanted to ask him about the woman in the photo, but one look at his creased face made her decide not to. Instead she asked, "Why don't you have a dog?" It had been bothering her for a while. Why would anyone who loved dogs as much as Wes did not have their own dog? She could hardly wait until she got a dog of her very own.

"What's this look like to you?" He pointed at Hazel, who lifted her snout and sniffed at his finger. Disappointed it wasn't a treat, she dropped her head back onto her paws.

"I meant a dog of your own," Jessie said.

"Owning a dog is a big responsibility."

"But you used to have a dog, didn't you?"

Wes glared at her. "Let's just get to the point of your little visit, shall we?"

"I was just asking—"

"And I'm just changing the subject. Now. I think it's time you learned the third Rule."

"Of the Ruff?" Jessie hopped from foot to foot, ready.

"Know when to leave it."

Jessie stopped hopping. "That . . . that's it?"

"Yes."

"Just know when to leave it?"

"Exactly. Couldn't have phrased it better myself."

"But that is how you phrased it."

"I know." Wes smiled. It looked brittle, like his face was cracking.

Jessie bit her lip. "But . . . leave what? How would I know?"

"Figure it out, kid." He leaned back in his chair and closed his eyes.

Jessie stood there, her excitement draining away slowly, like water through a clogged sink. "You're not planning on doing anything about that woman, are you?" she realized.

"Bingo. Give the kid a prize."

"But, she's stealing from you!"

"No, she's running a business. Same as I am. I hate it, too, but there's no sense getting all worked up about something like that. So I've decided," he opened his eyes, "to leave it."

"But . . . but it isn't fair."

"Neither's life. Besides, everyone leaves you eventually. What's it matter?" He closed his eyes again, one hand idly stroking Hazel's fluffy head. Eventually Hazel closed her eyes, too. It was like Jessie didn't exist, like it was her ghost standing there in that living room. So she grabbed her shoes and left. She was too much of a professional to slam the front door behind her, but she shut it very firmly. And then opened it and shut it again, just to be sure.

Know when to leave it. What a stupid rule. Jessie didn't believe in leaving anything, and she wasn't about to start now.

CHAPTER 12

Hey, you wanna go ride bikes?" Ann asked. It was Sunday afternoon; Jessie had spent the whole weekend sulking. Not that she considered it sulking. She didn't sulk. She was merely plotting. And avoiding Wes. And avoiding the park. And having absolutely no fun at all.

In fact, she was so bored she almost wouldn't mind hanging out with her cousin. And a bike ride sounded like a nice break. On the other hand, this was Ann-*Marie*. What if Jessie said yes, and then Ann made fun of her? She could almost hear her now: *Who even rides bikes anymore?*

"It's not exactly a hard question," Ann said.

Jessie narrowed her eyes. "What's the matter, now that Loralee's tired of you, you're bored and alone?"

Ann flushed. "You know, you could have just said no."

Jessie felt a strange twinge deep in her stomach as her cousin stalked away. Guilt? No, she didn't think so. She was probably just hungry.

But as she sat there, she kept seeing the way Ann's face had crumpled, and her stomach tightened and tightened until it was like a fist clenching. "Whatever," Jessie muttered. Ann deserved those words. Jessie knew she did. So she didn't apologize, and Ann didn't speak to her for the rest of the day.

The next morning Jessie was up and dressed before her alarm again. She had never been so relieved to get to a Monday.

Wes was sitting on his porch in his customary spot, sipping his customary tea. "You're early." He scowled.

"Isn't that a good thing?"

"No. It means I can't even enjoy my morning cup of tea in peace."

Jessie's steps slowed under the force of his irritation. She could feel it like it was a wave bearing down on her, and she suddenly remembered the way he'd told her not to bother him that weekend. Maybe her aunt and uncle were right, and she should just leave him alone.

Wes sighed and put his mug down on its coaster. "Might as well get this over with." He stood and disappeared inside his house.

Jessie danced from foot to foot, uncertain. Should she follow him inside? Go to the car? Just call today another bad day and crawl home?

Before she could make up her mind, Wes was back, a purple hip pack looped over his arm. Aside from the color and obvious newness, it looked just like his other one, with a wide elastic strap, a large zippered pouch in back, and a sturdy-looking clip in front. "Here." He thrust it at her.

"What?" Her heart raced faster than Angel out of the gate. "Is this . . . is that . . . am I . . . ?"

"If I'd known this would render you speechless, I'd have given you one a long time ago." He shook it. "Go on, take it. It's yours."

With trembling fingers, Jessie accepted the hip pack. "Does this mean," she whispered, "that I can actually walk some dogs now?"

"It does." Wes hesitated, then added, "We'll start you out with individual dogs, some of the easier ones, and see how you do. Then maybe a small pack or two."

Jessie hugged the hip pack to her chest, her eyes burning. "Thank you," she sniffed.

Wes shifted awkwardly. "Right. Well. Lots to do today." He brushed past her and unlocked his car. "Hurry it up, kiddo. I'm not paying you to stand around."

"You're not paying me at all, actually."

"And for good reason. Now get in the car."

Jessie smiled. She felt like a cloud, all light and fluffy and full of purpose. Before getting in the car, she adjusted the hip pack to fit her and then clipped it around her waist. She was official now. She was On The Job. Her poop-scooping days were a thing of the past.

"Hey, when you're done there, I have another pile for you," Wes called.

"But it came from one of *your* dogs. Why should I have to clean it up?"

"Because I don't want to." Wes chuckled. "Ah, the joys of bringing on some help."

Jessie fumed silently but cleaned up the dog poop. "Come on, Pickles," she told the black Aussie mix that was clipped to her hip pack. Wes clipped all leashes to his belt using a carabiner and had Jessie do the same thing. She was also supposed to keep a hand on the leash at all times. It felt a little awkward at first, but she was starting to get the hang of it. And as Pickles trotted along obediently next to her, she felt like a real dog walker, like she knew what she was doing.

"Hey! Who's walking who?" a random jogger called to her.

Jessie scowled. Did she not look in control here?

"Irritating, isn't it?" Wes muttered as the man jogged on. "You'll hear a constant rotation of about six different comments. That's one of the popular ones. Pay attention to the others. There will be a quiz later in the week."

"Really?"

Wes shrugged. "If I remember. Also here's another dog for you." He unclipped Bear. She took the leash and added it to her carabiner. Now she had a leash in each hand, and she could feel the dogs pulling her forward. She imagined herself as an old-fashioned carriage, powered by dogs instead of horses.

"Drop your weight. Keep that pack slung a little lower on your hips. And remember, watch out for squirrels," Wes instructed as she walked next to him. "Because if you don't see them first, you won't be prepared when your dogs see them. And see them they will." He smiled. "Especially Pickles."

Jessie nodded. She kept her energy calm and confident

and kept an eye out, paying close attention to her surroundings. They were in the park, making their way down the shaded elm tree path. As for the third Rule . . .

She noticed Max playing soccer in the field where they used to meet. He was with three other boys, plus, of course, Loralee. As if he sensed her, he turned, his eyes meeting hers. He grinned and lifted one hand in a friendly wave. Jessie did not return it. Instead, she looked past him at her enemy, narrowing her eyes on Loralee's smug face.

Know when to leave it. Yeah, right.

"Squirrel!" Wes warned.

Pickles lunged forward, and Jessie forgot all about Loralee and Max as she dropped her weight and pulled back on the leash.

"Let's see, there was, 'You sure have your hands full,' 'That's quite a pack,' 'Got room for one more,' and, uh, 'You need a sled.' I think those were the main ones," Jessie said. "Oh yeah, and the very clever 'Who's walking who?'" She still disliked that one the most.

"You're forgetting one." Wes handed her a water bottle.

Jessie drank slowly. She'd been officially walking dogs for four days now, each day hotter than the last. Today the humidity coated the world in sweat until it felt like she was breathing it in. She capped the empty bottle, and then remembered. "'Can I pet your dogs?'" That was the one *she* had said, back when she'd first seen Wes. Her face burned. She had been such an amateur. You were never supposed to interrupt a dog walker on the job like that. A civilian, sure. But a dog walker? Terrible form.

Wes grinned and tossed her a granola bar. "Good job, kid. And nice work today. Three dogs at once? I'm almost impressed."

"Thanks," Jessie muttered, still embarrassed. She *was* proud of herself, though. She'd managed to successfully walk Bear, Pickles, and Sammy the golden retriever. It took a while to figure out how to organize the leashes with only two hands, but eventually she'd managed to put Pickles and Sammy together on one side and Bear on her other side. Not bad for her first week actually walking dogs.

"Same time tomorrow?" Wes asked.

"Of course."

"Good. Because I think you're ready to try Angel again."

Jessie dropped her granola bar. "Really? You really think I'm ready?" Pride unfurled in her chest like a flag.

"Well, if you're not, at least I'll get a good show." He chuckled.

"That's not very nice," Jessie grumbled as she picked up her granola bar.

"I know. Now scram."

"What about Hazel?" She gave her granola bar a half-hearted brush and finished eating it. Five second rule. Besides, tonight it would be fish again for dinner. She needed all the decent food she could get before then.

"I'll go pick her up myself later." Wes pushed his sweaty hair back from his face. "Probably could do with a shower first."

"To pick up a dog?" Jessie thought of Hazel. And then she thought of Hazel's beautiful, fancy house, and beautiful, fancy owner, and she thought she was getting a glimmer of . . . something. Some sort of realization that she didn't want to examine too closely. It made her feel odd, like she was walking around in someone else's skin. It was simpler to think everything was about the dogs, and simpler was how she preferred things.

CHAPTER 13

May I please be excused?" Jessie asked. She'd eaten all her fish, which was a little better this time, and all the steamed asparagus, which was not.

"Sure," Uncle David said. "Run off and be free." He poked sadly at his own remaining asparagus and sighed.

"Me too?" Ann asked.

"Yes, yes." Uncle David fluttered a hand at both of them.

"Wait, Jessie, Ann-Marie," Aunt Beatrice said, and Jessie froze in a half crouch, her butt hovering a few inches off her chair. "Tomorrow we're going to a party."

"Ooh, a party?" Ann said. "Whose?"

"A friend of mine. She's new in town and is throwing what promises to be a huge affair." Aunt Beatrice's eyes glittered with excitement. "We'll be leaving at six P.M. sharp. I want you both showered and presentable."

"I'm always showered and presentable." Ann sounded offended.

"I know you are, Ann-Marie." Aunt Beatrice smiled at her daughter, then transferred that smile to Jessie, where it grew hard and brittle. Under its force, Jessie felt her unbrushed hair and remembered she was currently wearing the same shirt she'd slept in. "Be presentable," Aunt Beatrice repeated. "Six P.M., sharp."

Great. Jessie hated boring, stuffy adult parties. "Now may I be excused?" she asked.

Someone knocked on the front door.

"Fine," Aunt Beatrice said. "But go see who that is first. And David? Eat your asparagus, would you? It won't taste good cold."

"Don't see how it could taste worse," he muttered.

"David!"

"I meant, *mmm*, eating it now, and loving every bite!"

Jessie grinned as she opened the front door, then froze.

"Hello, Jessie," Loralee said. She pulled her glossy lips back in a smile that was more of a snarl. "Max sends his regards." Then she pushed past her, trilling for "Ann-Marie."

Jessie stood there, shaking. *Calm and confident energy,* she told herself. Then she turned and walked as quickly as she could past the kitchen.

"Of course you can get a ride with us to the party tomorrow," Ann was saying as Jessie hustled by. "Right, Mom?"

"We can make room," Aunt Beatrice decided.

Jessie's heart sank. One of her aunt's snooty friends *and* Loralee? That party tomorrow was sounding worse and worse.

She retreated into Ann's bedroom, but her solitude

didn't last long; a few minutes later Ann strolled in and flopped down on her bed. They hadn't exchanged more than a few frosty words in days, but Jessie couldn't resist asking, "Loralee gone already?"

"Yeah, she had to go. But we're going to hang out all day tomorrow." Ann's face practically glowed. Jessie looked away. She'd seen that same eager look on the faces of the dogs she walked.

"Sounds . . . fun," she whispered.

"Hey, maybe you can find Max tomorrow. I mean, he'll probably be free to play soccer again."

"No. I've already got plans," Jessie said shortly.

"Suit yourself." Ann pulled out a book, and Jessie let the silence thicken and envelop her.

"Are you ever going to tell me the next Rule?" Jessie asked as Wes drove them over to Angel's house the next morning. She'd been asking for Rule Number Four every day that week.

Wes sighed. "Be patient."

"Is that a Ruff Rule?"

"No, it's a life rule."

"Well, I've gotten this far without following it, so it can't be too important."

He rubbed the furrow between his eyebrows and muttered to himself, but Jessie knew she'd won. He usually did that before giving in. "Fine." He pulled into Angel's driveway. "The fourth Rule of the Ruff is this: Always be ready."

"'Always be ready'?"

"Yes. A dog is always ready. Time for a walk? He's ready. Time for a nap? He's ready. There's food? Ready. He never has to prepare for anything, because he has all he needs with him at all times."

"Or she," Jessie pointed out.

Wes scowled. "I'm using 'he' in the general sense."

"My dad says that's an outmoded form of usage. It should be 'him or her,' and 'he or she,' in order to be properly grammatical."

Wes's scowl deepened, a pulsing vein in his forehead joining the furrow between his eyebrows. "Do you want to walk this dog, or not?"

"Yes!" Jessie scrambled out of the car, then tightened her hip pack and checked that the leash was attached securely. This would be the real test. If she could successfully walk Angel, then she truly deserved to call herself a dog walker.

Wes got out more slowly. "Now, you remember what I taught you?"

"Yes."

"Knees bent, drop your weight, quick snap of the wrist to pull back on the leash if needed. Firm voice—"

"I remember," Jessie interrupted. "I'm ready. You might say I'm *always* ready." She grinned.

Wes's face twitched into the beginnings of a smile. Turning away from her, he opened the gate and Jessie followed him into the yard.

She'd come here with Wes often enough since her disastrous first walk, but somehow knowing she'd be the one to walk Angel this time made it all feel different.

There were the lovably mangled toys, there was the half-full water bowl in the corner, and there was the doghouse, empty.

Jessie frowned and spun around. Empty. The whole yard was empty. Angel was gone.

CHAPTER 14

Wes hammered on the front door.

"Maybe they're not home?" Jessie suggested, still looking around for Angel. The fence was pretty high; would he have been able to jump it? The gate had been locked. Or maybe . . . "Maybe they're taking Angel for a walk themselves?"

"No. They're home, they're always home. And they don't walk Angel."

"Why not?"

"Because they can't handle him." Wes pounded on the door again.

From inside, Jessie heard a woman's voice holler, "Bill, someone's knocking on the door!"

"So? What do you want me to do about it?" a man yelled back.

"Er, maybe this is a bad time," Jessie suggested, inching back.

"It's always a bad time," Wes said. "People." He shook his head in disgust, then straightened his shoulders and knocked again.

The door opened. ". . . do everything myself," a woman was saying. She was short and squat, with steel-gray hair cropped shorter than Jessie's. Jessie rather thought she resembled Angel; same wide face, large brown eyes, and drooping jowl line. When she saw Wes, the woman's cheeks immediately flushed pink, and she took a step back. "Oh. Uh, hello, Wes."

"Hello, Agatha." Wes's voice was polite, but it was impossible not to sense the impatience lurking beneath it, like a dog crouching behind a fence as the neighbor's cat walked along the top. "I expect you know why I'm here."

"Um, actually, I'm a bit confused," Agatha said, but she sounded nervous. "I could have sworn we told you we didn't need a walk today."

"No, you most assuredly did not."

"Bill!" she yelled.

"Coming, coming," a man's voice called, followed by slow, ominous footsteps. The door pulled all the way open to reveal an old man in a white tank top. Despite his hunched shoulders, he was tall, much taller than Wes, and his eyes glittered like shards of glass. "Wes." He nodded.

"Bill," Wes said, nodding back. Jessie shifted behind him, feeling awkward and invisible.

"Wes says you never told him today's walk was canceled," Agatha said.

"I didn't," Bill agreed. "That was supposed to be your job."

"My job? Why my job?"

"Because it was your decision. I said sure, fine, but you had to make the switch."

"You said no such thing!"

"Decided to go with the other dog walker, did you?" Wes said, stopping the argument in its tracks.

Bill cleared his throat. "Well, yes. Actually, that's pretty much it."

"May I ask why? I mean, I've been walking Angel for a long time, and you've never complained."

Bill's shoulders hunched a little farther. "Look, I think you do great with Angel, I really do, but—"

"Monique sends us pictures!" Agatha cut in. "Look!" She pulled out a very fancy phone and tapped a few buttons, then showed Wes something on the screen. Jessie craned around him to see.

Angel's huge pink tongue lolled over half the screen, his wide pit bull face scrunched around it in a smile. Next to the dog was the beautiful woman from before, also smiling. "A dog selfie," Jessie said. She hated to admit it, but it was a good picture.

"She did a trial walk yesterday afternoon," Bill said as Agatha took the phone back.

"Pictures," Wes said softly. "She sends you pictures."

"And cute little notes," Agatha added. "She said Angel was a good dog."

"I'm sorry, Wes." Bill looked down at the floor. "Thank you for your care. And, uh, we'll still pay you for today, of course."

"Don't bother. I don't want your money." Wes turned and strode from the porch.

"Well, that was a little rude. Don't you think that was a little rude?" Agatha asked her husband.

Bill shrugged. "I think, for Wes, that was very . . . restrained. He *has* been walking Angel for a long time."

"But still. He's *our* dog, and it's *our* choice."

"Your choice. I'd prefer to stick with Wes."

"Well," Agatha huffed. Then she seemed to notice Jessie for the first time. "And who are you?"

Jessie hesitated. She knew she should have followed Wes off the porch, but she couldn't just leave. She had to say something. Swallowing, she looked Agatha in the eye. "I think you're making a mistake."

"Who is she, Bill?" Agatha turned to her husband.

"How should I know?"

"I'm Wes's assistant. And he's a really good dog walker. I mean, he's not good at all the other stuff, the people stuff, but he's good with the dogs." Jessie's face burned and she began to wish she'd never opened her mouth, especially as Agatha peered at her like she was some sort of strange insect. Clearly, *she* wasn't very good at the people stuff, either. "Anyways. I thought you should know," she mumbled. And then she turned and ran back to the car. Like a coward, her tail between her legs.

Wes was already in the driver's seat. Jessie barely had time to jump into the back and shut the door before he was backing out of the driveway. They drove in complete and painful silence, until Wes pulled back into his own driveway.

"What about the rest of the dogs?" Jessie asked.

Wes tapped his fingers against the steering wheel. "I'll take care of them," he decided. "You go on home."

"What? Why? Did I do something wrong?"

"No. I just . . ." He sighed, his shoulders slumping. "I need to be alone with my dogs today. Please, just go away."

It was the "please" that did it. Jessie had never heard him say that word before, and his whole body sagged around it. It was like watching a dog who has just been dropped at the shelter, the moment he realizes the people he loves are driving away from him forever.

Jessie sniffed, unclipped her leash from her belt, and slid out of the car without another word. What could she possibly say to make him feel better? He'd lost so many dogs, and now Angel, too . . .

So she left him, sitting in his car, all alone. She felt so heavy, for once she couldn't even imagine herself as something else. She was just Jessie, defeated.

CHAPTER 15

Jessie found herself at the park, almost without realizing it. It was like her feet knew she wasn't ready to go home. It was overcast that morning, a perfect cool temperature. The dogs would really appreciate that.

She sighed and sat down under a tree, hugging herself. The dogs might appreciate it, but she was beginning to wish she'd worn something with long sleeves. She thought about running; running always warmed her up, and without any dogs to walk today, she could use the exercise. But she just sat there. Running took too much energy. Getting up took too much energy. Everything took too much energy.

"Angel, no. Heel. Heel!"

Jessie's unfocused gaze drifted across the park. There was Angel . . . she felt the shock of recognition like a punch to the stomach. Even though she'd been ready for it. Even though this must have been part of the reason her feet took her to the park: to see the other dog walker. Monique. She rolled the name around in her mind and tried not to like it.

Angel lunged after a squirrel, and Monique tripped and stumbled and cursed next to him. "Someone's not using calm, confident energy," Jessie whispered. But it didn't make her feel better. Well, maybe a little better.

"Jessie?"

Jessie looked up. And the world. Just. Stopped.

He wore a snug navy-blue shirt with white stripes on the sleeves, black shorts, and his normal ratty baseball cap pulled low.

"So it is you! It's been so long, I forgot what you looked like." He grinned, his sharp canines on full display.

Jessie's heart twisted in her chest. She was not prepared for this meeting. She needed time to remember how angry she was, and that was hard to do when Max was smiling his fox smile and acting so happy to see her. "Er," she managed.

"So, where've you been?" Max sat down next to her, his leg lightly brushing hers. Jessie hated that she noticed that.

"Er," she tried again, still mentally groping for that anger.

"I've had to find other soccer partners. But don't worry," he punched her lightly in the shoulder, "none of them are anywhere near as good as you."

"By other soccer partners, do you mean Loralee?" And just like that her anger was back. Jessie wrapped herself in it, imagining it as a fluffy blanket, soft and stifling.

"And other people, too," Max said defensively. "I don't spend all my time with her."

Jessie snorted.

"Hey, you ditched me. You can't exactly be angry at me."

Jessie gaped at him. "OK, first of all, I can be whatever I want to be, and second of all, I never ditched you! *You* ditched *me!* We were supposed to meet at the park, and you never showed."

"What? No! *You're* the one who didn't show. I might have been late, but you stopped coming altogether."

"Whatever," Jessie huffed, standing.

"And there you go again."

"Well, I'm sure you'll be too busy with your *girlfriend* to play anyhow."

"Actually, she's busy today, so I'm free."

Jessie noticed he didn't correct her terminology. "Girlfriend" loomed between them, larger and smellier than anything Jessie had ever had to clean up for Wes.

"I'm busy, too," she said.

"No, you're not. You're just sulking like a little girl."

"What?"

"Yeah, a little baby girl who's too scared to play me in soccer."

Jessie crossed her arms. "Your reverse psychology isn't going to work on me."

Max stood, too, and mirrored her pose. "No? Well, that's good, because I didn't want to play you in soccer anyhow."

"Yeah, you did. Admit it."

"If I admit it, will you play?"

"Yes."

"OK, then yeah, I did want to play you in soccer. You

can start." He grinned and tossed the ball at her, and Jessie caught it automatically.

"W-wait—"

"Too late! We made a deal." Max sprinted across the field, already turning his hat backward.

Jessie hesitated for another second and then had to admit grudgingly that he'd caught her. She'd play him; after all, it wasn't like she had anything better to do. But she would stay angry. She wasn't going to forget she was angry with him. Not for one single moment.

Jessie ducked left, circled right, and launched the ball. It sailed effortlessly past Max and through the goal. Victory. "Are you letting me win? Because this was just too easy," Jessie laughed.

Max went after the ball and dropped it in front of her. "That was just the warm-up game. Everyone knows it's the second game that really counts."

"Says who?"

"Everyone. Obviously." Max grinned. Then he looked past her, and his grin faltered.

"What?" Jessie glanced behind her. "Oh."

Loralee leaned against a tree, her body a sharp slash of irritation, from her tightly crossed arms to her tightly pressed lips to the *tap-tap-tap* of one of her tightly laced boots. "Finally noticed me?" she huffed.

"Uh, hey, Loralee," Max said. He glanced at Jessie, then away. "Er, I thought you were busy today?"

Loralee pushed away from the tree and stalked toward them, her hair swishing dangerously down her back. "I said I *might* be busy. Looks like you just jumped all over that opportunity." She bared her teeth in the worst excuse for a smile Jessie had ever seen. "But it turns out I'm completely free today. Isn't that *great*?"

Max frowned. "What's with the attitude?"

Loralee froze. And then it was like a shiver ran through her whole body, her icy expression melting away. "Oh, Max. You know I'm just playing around." This time her smile was wide and sweet and so very, very fake. There was no way Max was buying it. Right? But when Jessie snuck a peek at him, he was already relaxing, his easy grin sliding slowly into place.

"I just hope you're not too busy now for *me*," Loralee said. "You know, now that I went through all this trouble so we could spend the day together."

"Never too busy for you," Max said.

Jessie wanted to throw up. She should leave. She should sneak away. Now. But it was like her feet were stuck to the grass.

Max took his baseball cap off, ran a hand through his sweaty curls, and put the hat back on facing forward, a sure sign their soccer playing was over.

Loralee's gaze locked on Jessie, and all traces of her smile, fake or otherwise, vanished. "I'm sure *you*," Loralee jerked her chin at Jessie, "have better things to do than hang around with other people's boyfriends. Like, I don't know, dressing up as a fairy princess, or whatever?"

Jessie's face was a sun, scalding and hot and full of throbbing embarrassment. She unstuck her feet and silently marched away.

"You don't have to be so mean to her," she heard Max say, and she sped up. She didn't want to hear Loralee's response. She didn't want to hear Max's pity. She just wanted to go find a deep, dark hole somewhere and crawl inside forever.

Jessie was running by the time she got to the house. She slipped in through the back door and headed to her cousin's room, planning on burrowing under the blankets on her cot and imagining herself inside a cave, hidden away in the depths of Alaska, or South America, or somewhere else even farther away. The moon, perhaps.

She pushed open Ann's bedroom door and stopped short.

Ann was very pink; the rims of her eyes were pink, the tip of her nose was pink, and she had two little pink spots on her pale cheeks. "Oh, h-hey, Jess," Ann sniffed, surreptitiously wiping her eyes with the back of her hand. "I was just . . . I was . . ." She sniffed again. "Do you have a tissue?"

Jessie went to the bathroom for some toilet paper and brought it back.

Ann blew her nose noisily. "Sorry. I think I have a cold. Or a-allergies." She tried to smile. "Came on s-sudden." Her voice hitched in a little sob, and she buried her face in her wad of toilet paper.

Ann wore a large Hello Kitty shirt, her old favorite, and looked nothing like the Ann-Marie she'd been all summer. She looked . . . crushed. She looked like Wes after losing Angel, like a dog locked inside on a summer's day.

Jessie's insides thawed. "Loralee busy today?" she asked softly.

Ann sniffed and blew her nose again, then nodded. "S-something came up."

"I'll bet." Jessie pictured Loralee out on the field, staking her claim on Max. She hesitated. Ann had been a terrible excuse for a cousin, ditching her for Loralee again and again. If Loralee were here, Ann would be ditching her still. But she just looked so sad, so lonely, and Jessie found herself asking, "You wanna watch a movie or something?"

Ann looked up. "Really?"

"Sure."

"You're not busy with that dog guy?"

Jessie smiled. "No. Something came up."

Ann's smile was a little more genuine. "OK. I mean, if you want to."

"No romantic comedies," Jessie warned as she followed her cousin out of the room. "Nothing stupid, OK?"

"Yes, yes," Ann sighed. "I remember."

"He is definitely not the greatest character of all time," Ann said, rolling her eyes. "I don't know why you love these movies so much. They're so old."

"They're classics," Jessie said. "That makes them time-less. And he so is the greatest. Yippee-ki-yay—"

"Don't finish that. Mom will kill you."

Jessie grinned. "I wasn't going to finish it. I'm just saying John McClane is amazing."

"Well. I suppose he's OK. For a bald guy."

"I am going to ignore that snide remark and start movie three." Jessie was just about to push play when her uncle wandered into the living room.

"*Die Hard* marathon, is it?" he asked.

"You bet," Jessie said. "Want to join us?" She knew that while Ann only secretly loved these movies, her uncle was a wholehearted supporter.

"Save me," Ann muttered, but she didn't get off the couch.

"I'd love to join you ladies, but unfortunately I have to put a stop to the movie watching. Bea wants you to get dressed and ready for the party."

"Already?" Jessie whined.

"Already? Jessie, it's five P.M."

"Is it really?" Ann shot off the couch. "I have to get ready!" She dashed toward her room, Jessie reluctantly following.

"What's the rush?" Jessie asked as her cousin rummaged around in her closet.

"Loralee said she'd swing by early."

Jessie felt cold suddenly. "She's still coming with us?"

"Of course she is. Why wouldn't she?"

"Well, she was supposed to hang out with you today, too. And then she bailed. You really want to bring her to some stupid party?"

"She didn't bail. Something important came up."

"She wanted to hang out with Max! She bailed on you to hang all over him instead!"

"That's not true."

"I saw her at the park, Ann."

Ann narrowed her eyes. "It's Ann-Marie."

Jessie shook her head. She didn't say anything else to her cousin as they took turns showering and getting dressed. Instead, she let the wall rise back up between them. She imagined it rising higher and higher, locking the old version of Ann away forever, trapping her behind this new Ann-Marie.

As the minutes ticked away, though, Loralee didn't show up. And when six P.M. rolled around, and still no Loralee, Jessie started to relax. Maybe she'd bailed. Again. Jessie pictured her curled up on the couch, draped all over Max, his arm around her shoulders . . .

Argh. Now she kind of wanted Loralee to be *here* instead.

No, no she didn't. Of course, she didn't.

"What's wrong with you?" Ann asked.

Jessie realized she was pacing and stopped herself. "I'm deep in thought."

"No wonder your face is all scrunched up. Must be painful."

Jessie stuck out her tongue, and Ann mirrored her.

"Maturity, Ann-Marie, show a little maturity," Aunt Beatrice sighed. She glanced at Jessie but just shook her head, like she knew those words would be wasted there. "Is that really what you're wearing?" she asked instead.

"What? I'm showered and presentable, exactly as promised." Jessie ran her fingers through her damp curls. She had even put on her best pair of jeans. Shorts would be too casual. But as Uncle David wandered in wearing a button-down shirt and tie, Jessie began to get uncomfortable. Just how fancy was this party? Sure, Ann and Aunt Beatrice were wearing dresses, but they liked to dress up. Her uncle hated it.

It didn't matter. Jessie hadn't brought any nicer clothes, and there was no way she was borrowing anything from Ann.

"She's fine, Bea," Uncle David said. "In fact, I'm losing the tie in solidarity." And he ripped it from around his neck and tossed it on the couch.

"David!" Aunt Beatrice snapped.

"What can I say? Jessie and I are rebels." He winked.

Aunt Beatrice sighed again, loud and dramatic, but before she could say anything, Ann's phone beeped. "Loralee?" Aunt Beatrice asked.

Ann read her text, her shoulders slumping. "She said she'd meet us there."

Aunt Beatrice's nostrils flared, but she didn't say anything bad about Loralee. She *never* said anything bad about Loralee. Jessie followed her aunt outside, mulling that over.

Loralee was not very nice. But somehow, she'd managed to get everyone wrapped around her glossy little fingers. Ann was trying to turn into her, Max couldn't get enough of her, and Aunt Beatrice would obviously switch Jessie out for Loralee in a heartbeat. Why? Why did everyone like her so much?

As Jessie got into the back seat of the car, she couldn't help but wonder if maybe it wasn't that they liked Loralee *more* but that they just liked Jessie *less*.

It was a terrible thought, a lonely thought, but she couldn't get rid of it, and the entire drive she could feel it pressing her down, down, into a tinier version of herself.

They parked on the street outside of a brightly lit

house. Noise spilled from the open windows, reaching for them with long tentacles of high-pitched laughter and boring conversation. As they walked to the door, Jessie and Ann exchanged looks, and for a second Jessie felt that connection with her cousin again. They were going to be stuck together at some stuffy party full of adults. And neither of them could stop it.

Her aunt rang the doorbell, then smoothed down the front of her dress and waited.

The door opened, and Jessie's stomach dropped. Standing there, framed in the doorway, was Monique.

The Enemy.

CHAPTER 16

Beatrice!" Monique gushed, stepping outside and exchanging one of those awkward fake adult hugs with Jessie's aunt. "So glad you could make it!" She wore a slinky black shirt with a ruffle along the top and a long blue and silver skirt that swished as she moved. Her hair was still in hundreds of small braids, but she'd twisted half of them up into a knot. Next to Aunt Beatrice, with her flouncy floral sundress and overly teased hair, Monique looked more like a supermodel than ever.

Jessie could hardly believe someone so beautiful could be so evil. But she knew behind those lovely cheekbones and that wide smile was a dog-walking thief.

"And this must be your husband." Monique turned the force of her smile onto poor Uncle David, whose ears went red immediately. "I've heard so much about you, Don."

"D-David."

"Oh. Right. Yes." Monique turned her smile up a notch. "Please, come in, come in." She disappeared inside.

"Maybe I should have worn that tie," Uncle David

muttered. Aunt Beatrice shot him a jagged look. "Kidding, Bea. Kidding," he said, following her inside.

"You coming?" Ann asked Jessie.

"I haven't decided yet."

Ann rolled her eyes and left Jessie there on the doorstep. It was still light out, the chill of night just starting to coat the air, the first few fireflies lighting up in the front yard.

Jessie sighed, then eased herself inside, closing the door behind her.

Immediately, the noise and heat of way too many people enveloped her, and she felt like she might suffocate. Was the whole town here? For a stupid party? Why? Just how many people did Monique know?

Jessie slunk down the hall. It opened into a large dining room with hardly any furniture. No tables or chairs, just a counter covered in different bite-size foods. Jessie ducked around laughing adults and snagged a ham-and-cheese wrap and a couple of cupcakes. She was just reaching for a shrimp when a giant poster behind the food caught her eye.

In bold purple letters were the words "Monique's Buddy Walks!" And beneath that, in italicized script, it read, "First walk free," with a little stylized illustration of a woman walking a pack of dogs.

Jessie dropped her shrimp back onto the tray, her appetite gone.

"Hey, you can't just put food back, you know," a woman scolded her. "That's rude."

Jessie started to apologize to the woman and then recognized her as Angel's owner. "You," she said.

The woman blinked. "Do I know . . . oh." Obviously she'd just recognized Jessie, because she mumbled some excuse and shuffled away. As Jessie watched her go, she suddenly realized: This room was full of dog owners. Words filtered through the general noise, names like Rover and Mr. Fluff-butt, names that had to belong to dogs. This was a trap, this whole entire party, with the fancy food and the free wine.

All these people were targets for Monique. All these people, and their dogs.

How was her aunt friends with this woman? How could this happen?

"Cute posters, aren't they? It's my sister's design."

Jessie looked up, and suddenly she was face-to-face with *her*. With Monique. "Uh . . ." Jessie swallowed. This was terrible. She had to escape!

"Hey," Monique said slowly, her eyes widening. "I know you."

Oh no! Jessie froze.

"You were running with that pit bull. I remember I was so impressed with your reflexes. You're friends with Max, right?"

"Uh . . ." That seemed to be all Jessie could say.

"Monique, tell Rebecca here about your sister," a woman cut in, and Jessie recognized her stick-straight blond hair and sharp nose. Sweetpea's owner. The first traitor. "She doesn't believe me."

"Your sister seriously walks dogs for Bianca? Like, the singer, Bianca?" the woman's friend asked, gesturing wildly with her half-empty wine glass.

"Oh yes." Monique turned away from Jessie. "My sister is famous. A celebrity dog walker."

A celebrity dog walker? Was that a real thing? Shaking her head, Jessie backed away. And *that pit bull?* As if Monique didn't know exactly who Angel was. What a faker! Still, that was close, too close. Jessie had to get out of here. Maybe she could sit outside until her aunt was ready to leave.

She paused to grab one more cupcake. Her appetite might be gone, but these cupcakes had thick chocolate icing *and* raspberry filling. She snuck a quick glance around the room, then peeled the wrapper off and stuffed the whole thing in her mouth.

"I saw that."

Jessie turned. It took her a second to recognize the boy in front of her; he looked strange without his normal hat, and wearing a polo shirt, of all things.

"One bite, huh? Impressive," Max said.

Jessie chewed, chewed, swallowed.

"You have chocolate all over your mouth."

She used her sleeve to hurriedly wipe the crumbs off her face. "Thanks," she said. Then she remembered the last time she'd seen him, how he'd dropped her for Loralee that morning, and suddenly that cupcake felt like a lump of rage in her stomach. "Shouldn't you be glued to your girlfriend's side, as usual?"

Max's eyes widened. "I am not—"

"There you are!" Loralee materialized at his side, practically glowing as she clutched possessively at his arm.

Max's cheeks flared bright red.

"Yeah, that's what I thought," Jessie said. She turned her back on both of them and slid through the crowd. She'd had enough Max and Loralee time for the day. And as she dodged elbows and avoided trampling feet, Jessie realized she'd had enough people time in general.

She remembered what Wes had said, the day he agreed to teach her the Rules of the Ruff: *The whole reason I became a dog walker was so I wouldn't have to deal with people.* Right here, surrounded by shrill laughter and loud conversations, Jessie suddenly understood what he meant; she had never felt more alone in her life. Dogs were way better company. They didn't lie or make snide comments or gossip. They were easy to understand. They wouldn't pretend to be your friend and then ditch you for Loralee.

She thought of the glossy posters, of Monique's "celebrity dog walker" family and beautiful smile, the way she could move to a new town and a month later throw the kind of party that everyone came to. How effortlessly she could get people to like her. Loralee was just like that. People liked her even when she was mean to them. Even when she didn't care about them at all.

And then Jessie thought of Wes, who was unpleasant and grumpy and would have been as comfortable at this party as a dog at a fireworks show. Wes, who cared more about dogs than anyone she knew, and who was losing those dogs, one by one, until he really would be alone.

Jessie clenched the cupcake wrapper in one fist. She had to do something. Wes was wrong about Rule Number Three: There was *never* a good time to leave it. And she was here, in the lair of their enemy. There had to be some-thing here she could use to their advantage. Maybe if she looked through Monique's dog walking supplies she'd find . . . what? Jessie wasn't sure, exactly. Some proof that Monique was a faker? That she didn't understand the first thing about dog walking or the Rules of the Ruff?

Jessie mulled it over as she tossed her cupcake wrapper in the gleaming trash can. Monique's car would be the best place to look. She probably kept most of her leashes and things in there. And even if Jessie didn't find anything she could use against the other dog walker, it would be good to at least know exactly what she and Wes were up against.

The more Jessie thought about it, the more she liked that idea. She'd be taking action to help Wes and escaping this stuffy party. No one was paying attention to her, so she slipped down the hall and snuck outside. The sun had just begun creeping below the horizon, spilling red and purple in vibrant waves across the evening sky.

Jessie quietly closed the front door behind her and walked over to the dark green Subaru parked at the top of the driveway. Her shoulder blades prickled. Any second now Monique would spring outside and catch her. Or her aunt would. Or someone.

Jessie forced herself to breathe slowly. Calm and confident. She checked her surroundings; no one was outside. Now was her chance. Peering in through the car window, she noticed the tangle of leashes sprawled across the back seat, the roll of doggie poop bags beneath it. Definitely Monique's car.

Jessie reached for the door handle, then hesitated. What was she even planning here? She'd be in so much trouble if she got caught.

But when she pictured Wes without any dogs, her chest filled with that same familiar ache she got whenever she thought of her mom, like her heart was bleeding. She'd felt like that at the end of last summer, too, when Ann discarded her as easily as she'd shuck off an ugly sweater. That terrible, endless longing, the way it throbbed and throbbed inside until some days all Jessie could think of was what had been. She didn't want to feel that way ever again, and she wasn't going to let Wes go through that, either.

Monique couldn't be allowed to win. Not this time.

Jessie made up her mind; there was no turning back now.

She grabbed the door handle. Locked. But the front window was rolled down far enough for a skinny twelve-year-old arm to snake in and pull up the lock. Jessie held her breath as she opened the car door. No car alarm. She relaxed a little and slipped inside, hardly believing she was doing this.

She glanced up at the house. The front door was still firmly shut, but she knew she didn't have a lot of time before someone noticed she was missing. She had to move quickly, efficiently. She imagined herself as a spy, on a top-secret mission of international importance. She was doing recon for the Ruff. Immediately, Jessie's chest loosened and she felt a lot better. Spies weren't nervous about breaking into someone else's car. Spies didn't feel guilty. They just did their job and got out.

Quietly humming the theme song to *Mission: Impossible*, she did a quick search of the car. The back seat had four leashes, the half-unrolled poop bags she'd seen from outside, plus another two rolls that were still sealed up, and a mangled tennis ball. The seat was partially covered by a blue-and-gray quilt liberally speckled with dog fur. In the front, Jessie found a small stash of granola bars (the gross kind with raisins instead of chocolate chips), a half-empty bottle of water, and a collapsible dog dish. Nothing too nefarious. Yet.

She scooted over to the front passenger seat and opened the glove compartment. Immediately, a cascade of crumpled receipts and papers tumbled into her lap. "Oh, no," Jessie whispered, grabbing them and trying to stuff them back in. It was like trying to shovel an avalanche back up a mountain; the more stuff she jammed back into the compartment, the more tumbled out around her. Now there were other things mixed in with the paper: a couple of pens, a hair tie, two packs of gum, a spare key, and a potato chip bag.

Jessie glanced over at the house, just in time to see the front door opening. Her heart leapt into her throat, and she worked desperately, using one hand to gather the mound of junk and cram it into the compartment while her other hand blocked everything from tumbling out again.

She closed it, shoving it until it latched, and then noticed the spare key was still out. Jessie groaned and picked it up. It looked like a car key, heavy and solid in her hand.

"—fresh air with me," a voice said. Max's voice. "It's too stuffy in there."

Jessie's fingers clenched around the key and she dove into the back seat, then over the top of it, grabbing the quilt and rolling it over her as she settled in the trunk. Had he seen her? She squeezed her eyes shut and waited.

"Don't be gone too long," a woman's voice said. Monique's voice. Jessie hated to admit it, but it was a lovely voice, deep and smooth and lilting. Hard to believe the owner of that voice kept a mountain of junk crammed inside her car. Just went to show you could never tell about a person.

"We won't be," Loralee's voice. Much less pleasant.

Next thing Jessie knew, Loralee and Max were stomping even closer to the car, Loralee prattling on about something or other. ". . . don't really feel like walking to the park," she was saying.

"Well, where else would we go?" Max asked.

"I was thinking of somewhere a little closer . . ." Loralee purred. Jessie could hear the click as the front door opened. "And look at that, it's unlocked. Must be fate."

CHAPTER 17

Jessie held her breath.

"The car?" Max asked. "Why would we—"

Sounds trickled over to Jessie's ears. Slurping sounds. Disgusting sounds. *Kissing* sounds. Jessie froze. Her ears burned and she tried to close them, but it was impossible.

"The car sounds good," Max said a few minutes later, his voice wobbly.

Loralee chuckled. "I thought you'd agree."

There was the sound of cloth moving against seats, and more disgusting kissing noises. Jessie tried hard not to picture it, but her imagination was already painting images of Max pressed up against Loralee, of their lips mashed together. Jessie tried not to breathe, not to think. This was a terrible idea. She should have just stayed inside; being trapped in the car where Loralee and Max were making out was worse than any party would have been.

"Ahem."

Jessie jumped. Was she caught? She felt equal parts terrified and relieved.

"Weren't you supposed to be getting fresh air?" Monique asked, and Jessie realized she wasn't the one who was caught, after all.

"Sorry, Monique," Loralee said, her voice small and contrite. What a faker. The door opened. Were they leaving? Please say they were leaving, Jessie prayed.

"Go on ahead, Loralee. I want to have a word with my son."

Darn it. Jessie rested her head against the floor of the trunk and listened to the sounds of Monique settling herself into the car, the door closing behind her. A long, tense, superawkward moment later, Max said, "Well? What did you want to say?"

"I'm not about to scold you—" Monique began.

"Good. Because I'm not doing anything wrong," Max huffed. "I'm settling in, just like you wanted."

"And I'm so proud of you," Monique said. "Loralee seems like a nice girl."

Jessie thought she might throw up. *Nice?* Seriously?

"I don't want to talk about it," Max said sullenly.

Monique sighed. "Look, I didn't want to move here, either. But your grandmother needs us, and Aunt Grace was right about the dog-walking business. It's easy money."

Easy money? *Easy* money? Jessie already had calluses developing on her palms from holding multiple leashes, her hip still ached from a walk two days ago when Pickles had done a flying leap at a squirrel, and she'd lost track of the number of bruises and scrapes she'd gotten during enthusiastic dog greetings. And that wasn't even counting the *real* work: somehow paying attention to the dogs *and* her surroundings while remaining calm and confident. Wes made it look effortless, but Jessie knew by now that properly walking a pack of dogs was about as "easy" as Loralee was "nice."

"So business is picking up?" Max asked, voice strained.

"Business is definitely picking up," Monique said. "I just signed two new clients tonight, in fact." She laughed. "Grace's suggestion of dog pictures and report cards was genius; the people around here are practically begging me to take their dogs out. At this rate, Wes will be folding up his business in no time. I'd almost feel bad for him, if he wasn't so unpleasant."

"I guess that means we really are staying."

"Yes, honey, we really are staying."

Silence filled the car, as thick as the icing on Monique's cupcakes. Jessie wanted to scream into it. Instead, she bit down on her knuckles.

"So . . . is that all you wanted to talk to me about?" Max asked finally.

"Well, I thought maybe you might want to help me—"

"You said it was easy," Max said sharply. "So why would you need help?"

"It *is* easy. I mean, it should be. They're just dogs. It's just walking."

Jessie couldn't feel the quilt around her, or the scratchy surface of the trunk beneath her cheek. She couldn't feel anything at all, just the hard planes of those terrible words: *They're just dogs.*

"But I'm still not used to walking more than one or

two at a time," Monique continued. "Having an assistant would be a huge help."

"I told you no. I'm not helping you walk dogs." The door opened again.

"I wasn't asking about you. I was thinking maybe your friend—"

The door slammed shut, cutting her off. Jessie let out a breath. She was alone again. Finally. She lay there a long time listening to the thumping of her heart and the memory of those words repeating over and over in her head: "At this rate, Wes will be folding up his business in no time." There was no denying what it meant. Monique wasn't just taking a few dog clients. No, she was planning to take them all. This wasn't just an invasion; it was a hostile takeover.

She had to warn Wes. And unpleasant? *Unpleasant?* OK, yes, Wes might not be the friendliest person, but the contempt in Monique's voice when she called him that . . . Jessie grit her teeth. That woman had no right to call Wes anything. At least he didn't pretend to be nice and then insult people behind their backs.

Jessie slowly crawled out of the car. She'd tell Wes first thing in the morning.

But when she opened Monique's front door, the sound of all those people smacked her in the face, the smell of too much perfume swirled all around her, and she froze on the doorstep. Across the room, she could just make out that large poster, the one that read "Monique's Buddy Walks!" and beneath it in smaller letters, "First walk free."

They're just dogs.

Something inside Jessie broke, shattering like her mug the day Ann left her, and she knew she couldn't go back inside. She couldn't, and she wouldn't.

She took one last look at the stylized picture of a woman walking a pack of dogs, and then she turned around, closing the door behind her.

Just dogs.

Monique didn't deserve them. She didn't deserve *any* of them. And Jessie wasn't going to let her take them away.

CHAPTER 18

Jessie knocked hard on Wes's door and then put her hands on her knees and gasped for breath. After sneaking away from Monique's house and wandering around for a few heart-stopping moments, she'd recognized Zelda's house a few blocks down. Thanks to Rule Number Two she knew how to get back to Wes's from there, but while it hadn't seemed like such a far distance when she'd ridden in Wes's car, on her own two feet, it was a whole different story.

Still, she'd made it. She was here.

The door stayed closed. Straightening, Jessie pounded on it again. She thought she could hear voices inside, and then a now-familiar howl. Hazel was here? How often did Wes petsit that little beast?

She pressed her ear to the door. Definitely voices. It sounded like Wes and a woman. Jessie was suddenly intensely curious. She couldn't picture Wes having someone over for dinner. Well, maybe a couple of dogs. But a person?

Finally, the door opened a crack and Wes's large nose

poked out, followed by the rest of his grumpy face. "You. Of course it's you."

"Who else would it be?"

"Who else indeed." He looked her up and down. "You look like you've been running."

"I have," Jessie said solemnly. "All the way from Zelda's house."

Wes's eyebrows rose. "That's a good three miles from here."

"Felt like ten."

He sighed. "I'd shut you out, but I have a feeling you'd keep knocking. And since you ran all this way," he glanced behind him, then stepped outside and pulled the door shut, "go ahead."

"Who's inside?"

"Hazel."

"Besides Hazel?"

Wes grimaced and made a point of starting the timer on his watch. "I'm giving you three minutes to tell me whatever it is. Starting . . . now."

"Three minutes? But I just ran all the way here and it's really import—"

"Two minutes fifty seconds."

Jessie sighed. "Fine," she grumbled, but she launched into her story. She knew she didn't have a lot of time, but she still had to mention a few details about the fancy party, ending with Monique's proclamation and then her own daring escape back here.

"Not sure I needed to hear about the cupcakes or your little teen drama—"

"I'm not a teen," Jessie reminded him. "And it was disgusting. They were making out right in front of me. And Loralee is so, so . . ." She shuddered. "Right in front of me."

"That does sound truly terrible."

"It was so much worse than terrible. It was—"

"Yes, yes." Wes waved that off. "But the rest of your story was useful."

"Really?"

Wes nodded. "Oh yes."

"Does that mean we're not going to leave it anymore?"

His eyes narrowed. "No. If it's a dogfight that woman wants, it's a dogfight she'll get." He stared off across the lawn, almost as if he were searching for Monique across the distance, his nostrils flaring. Then, abruptly, he looked back down at Jessie. "And you have this key still? The spare to her car?"

Jessie nodded and showed it to him.

Wes's smile was a terrifying thing. It was like watching a cobra spread its hood. Jessie involuntarily took a step back.

"That might help," he said softly, taking the key from her. "That might help a lot."

"H-help with what?"

If anything, his smile grew more terrifying. The cobra rearing back, about to strike. "Come back here Monday morning. Sunrise. We'll come up with a plan then."

"Monday?" Jessie asked, but Wes was already turning his back on her. "Sunrise?" she tried next. He opened the front door. "What kind of plan?" she added.

He glanced back at her. "You'll see."

"But—"

His timer beeped. "Ah, that'll be your time. Good night, Jessie." He shut the door.

Jessie stared at it. "Good night," she whispered. It was the first time Wes had called her by her name, instead of "kid." She wasn't sure what that meant, but it made her nervous. Still, Wes was going to fight back. Finally. He'd fight back, and she'd help, and good would triumph over evil. Their dogs would return.

The whole way back to Ann's house, Jessie tried thinking of a good plan for Monday. When she got inside the house, however, and found her aunt and uncle waiting for her, she realized she should have been working on a plan for tonight. Her aunt's face was redder than she'd ever seen it before, and even Uncle David's customary cheerful expression had been replaced by a grim mask.

"Hey, Aunt Bea, Uncle David." Jessie tried on a weak grin. "How was the rest of the party?"

CHAPTER 19

O f course you're grounded," Ann said. "You're lucky you're not murdered."

"But I can't be grounded! I need to go see Wes on Monday." Jessie flopped onto her cot, the back of one hand pressed against her forehead.

"Don't be so dramatic."

Jessie didn't dignify that with a response. She wasn't being dramatic enough, in her opinion. Here Wes was finally going to fight back, and she wouldn't even be able to help. This was a terrible thing. A travesty. An insurmountable obstacle.

Ann sighed. "This is your own fault, you know. If you'd just stayed at the party—"

"Blech," Jessie said.

Ann gave her a flinty-eyed stare. Jessie had never really understood that expression before, but now she could see it: merciless. "As I was saying," Ann continued after a long, cold moment, "if you'd just stayed, it would have been over soon and no big deal. Honestly, what were you even thinking, running away like that?"

"I wasn't running *away*! I was running *to*. I had life-or-death information that just couldn't wait."

"Still being dramatic, Jessie."

Jessie shrugged, which wasn't easy to do lying down. "I just . . . I had to leave. I can't explain it, but I just . . . had to." She sat up. "I'm sorry it meant you had to leave early, too, though. I know you wanted to hang out with Loralee."

Now it was Ann's turn to shrug. "She would have just spent the whole time talking to Max anyhow."

Jessie could still remember the horrible sucking noises of Max and Loralee making out in the car, and she grimaced. "Stupid Max."

"Stupid Max," Ann agreed. "Things were much simpler when he wasn't around."

That made Jessie think. "You know . . ." she said slowly, "it sounds like they were thinking they might have to leave."

"Who? Max?"

"Max and his mom. If the dog-walking thing didn't work out for them." Jessie fiddled with the edge of the blanket beneath her, trying to decide if she could trust Ann. "If you help me . . ."

"If I help you . . . what?"

Jessie hesitated.

"Oh, just spit it out. I'm tired and I want to go to sleep."

"If you help me get out of this grounding, I can help drive Max out of here."

Ann frowned. "How so?"

So Jessie told her. Not everything, but just enough. About how Monique was stealing Wes's dogs. And about how she was going to help Wes get them back.

Ann's frown deepened until she began to resemble Wes. "I'm not sure that's the best way to handle this."

"It's the only way I know," Jessie said. "The only way I can think of."

"And Wes is OK with this plan? What if you get caught? You'd be in a lot of trouble."

"I can take it." Jessie tried to sound brave, but already she was worried she'd gone too far, just leaving the party. What if her aunt told her dad, and he decided she wasn't mature enough for a dog of her own? That made her so sad that her eyes burned, and she had to turn away and rub at them. "I need to help Wes."

"Is it really that important to you?" Ann asked softly.

Jessie couldn't look at her; she was afraid she was going to start crying, so she just nodded.

"OK," Ann said. "I'll see what I can do."

"Y-you will?"

"Don't sound so surprised. I'm not *that* heartless." Ann flicked off the lights. "Now go to sleep. I'll talk to Mom in the morning."

But Jessie couldn't sleep. She was sure she'd be awake all night . . .

". . . ssie. Jessie. Jessie!"

"What? Where? It wasn't me!" Jessie sat up so fast her pillow slid off the cot and bounced on the floor.

"Well. I can see someone has a guilty conscience. As she should," Aunt Beatrice said, her whole face pinched and narrow and judging.

"S-sorry," Jessie mumbled, looking down.

Her aunt sighed. "Ann told me that you really need to go to work on Monday. And while I think you should be grounded from now until the day you leave for college, I agree that it's important to uphold prior commitments. Something you desperately need to learn."

Jessie tried to follow this long, vaguely offensive speech, molding her features into a mask of apology.

"So," Aunt Beatrice continued, "I'll consider ungrounding you Monday."

"You will?" Ann must have worked some serious magic.

"I'll *consider* it," her aunt repeated, "if . . ."

Jessie's heart sank. "If?" she squeaked.

"If you do everything I tell you to do this weekend. I have a lot of chores to be done: laundry to be washed and folded, corners to be dusted, boxes to be moved and organized. And you have a lot of energy and time on your hands." Aunt Beatrice actually smiled. It was not an improvement. "You work hard for me this weekend, and maybe, just maybe, you'll earn back your freedom." She stuck her hands on her hips. "Do we have ourselves a deal?"

Jessie thought it sounded like a pretty terrible deal, but she knew it was the best she'd get. "Yes, Aunt Beatrice."

"Then you'd better get up, get dressed. Meet me downstairs in five minutes."

Ann slipped inside after her mom left. "Well, I talked to her," she said cheerfully.

"I noticed."

Ann shifted her weight back and forth. "I mean, it won't be a fun weekend, I know."

"No, it won't." Jessie dug in her bag for a T-shirt and a pair of cotton athletic shorts.

"But it was the best I could do."

Jessie paused and looked up at her cousin. She realized there was something Ann was waiting for. Something she deserved. Jessie sighed. "Thank you, Ann," she mumbled.

Ann smiled sweetly. "You're very welcome."

And for some reason, Jessie smiled, too. She could picture the gap between them shrinking. It was still there, but now she could almost see the other side, her cousin's side, and it wasn't as awful as she'd thought. Maybe Ann could still be her cousin, after all.

A few hours later, Jessie had changed her mind. "She's no cousin of mine," she grumbled. "No cousin at all."

"Jessie!" her aunt called. "There's another load in the dryer for you!"

Jessie shook her head, then pictured the dogs. She was doing this for them. It would be over soon enough . . . It had to be.

CHAPTER 20

Jessie knocked softly at Wes's door for the third time. Finally, he opened it. "What are you doing here so early?" he demanded. "Sun's barely up."

"You told me sunrise."

"Did I?" Wes scratched at his head. "Well, I'm sure I didn't mean it. Come back later."

Jessie moved faster than he did, sticking her foot in the way of the door. She'd had a lot of practice with that move this summer. "Do you have any idea what I had to go through to get here?" she said. "I'm here, and I'm staying."

Wes's lips twitched. It was almost a smile, but then it was gone before Jessie could really be sure. "Fine. I suppose we do have a battle plan to come up with. Give me five minutes, and I'll meet you at the car."

Seven minutes later, they were on their way.

"Take these." Wes tossed a grungy baseball hat and a battered paperback book on the back seat with Jessie.

"Uh, thanks? You shouldn't have?" Jessie gingerly picked them up as Wes backed out of the driveway. The book was some kind of weird science-fiction novel that looked like it had been written a million years ago. Pretty cool spaceship on the cover, though, she decided.

"They're part of your disguise," Wes said. "You'll be observing the enemy today, and I don't want you spotted. Now, remember the Rules. Calm, confident energy; be aware of your surroundings; know when to leave it; and always be ready. These all apply to reconnaissance as much as to dog walking."

"I never knew dog walkers were really just spies in training."

Wes's scowl deepened. "Do you want to do this, or don't you?"

"Of course, I want to."

"Then stop being ridiculous."

Jessie tried, but she couldn't stop herself from saying, "Double O Seven, dog walker and government agent, reporting for duty."

"What did I say about being ridiculous?"

"Not to be?" Jessie grinned. She couldn't help it. She was nervous and excited and all jittery. She felt like someone had stuffed her full of bubbles, and it was hard to stop them bursting out.

Wes rubbed the furrow between his eyes. "Just use your head. Be smart. Think like a dog." He parked near Elm Park, then twisted to face her. "I'll be nearby."

"You're not joining me?"

"Someone still needs to walk these dogs. This is a solo mission. You got that?"

"Yes, sir." She saluted.

He shook his head. "Get out of my car."

Jessie opened her door and slid out, but Wes called her back before she took two steps.

"You're sure about this, kid?" He looked her up and down, his scowl gone, face serious.

Jessie felt some of the bubbles in her deflating under the weight of that stare. She nodded.

"OK. OK." Wes sighed. "Be careful. I'll see you back at the house this afternoon." Then he took off, leaving Jessie at the edge of the park, alone and on her first covert mission.

She stared at the car until Wes turned a corner, and then she shook herself. It was time to get to work. Time to think like a dog. A dog that was also a spy. A spy dog. Jessie smiled, then headed over to the row of elm trees and found a seat on a bench near the end of the row. She pulled Wes's old baseball cap low on her head and opened the book.

This first part was simple. She just had to sit here and study Monique's movements. They knew the other dog walker would be at the park soon; it was the best place to walk dogs in this town. Jessie would keep track of which dogs she walked, how she walked them, what supplies she used, and anything else they might be able to use against her. It was a good chance for her to really practice the second Rule of the Ruff and be aware of her surroundings.

Jessie waited.

The sun crawled slowly higher in the sky, the heat of the day rising around her.

She waited some more.

Sweat trickled down her back, bugs buzzed nearby, and absolutely nothing else happened. She started counting down seconds, then tried to read a page of her book, then stared up at the birds chirping nearby. Nothing, nothing, nothing.

Jessie sighed. This was going to be harder than she'd thought.

A dog barked.

Jessie practically leapt off her bench. Finally! But . . . it wasn't Monique. Just some random person walking . . . "Aww, is that a pug? Can I pet her? What's her name?"

"*His* name is Pugsley."

"A pug named Pugsley?" Jessie giggled.

The woman's eyes narrowed, her face scrunching until she resembled her dog. It wasn't a good look on a human. "Actually, he is Sir Pugsley the Seventh."

"The Seventh? So . . . there's been six other Pugsleys?" Jessie scratched just above his little curled tail. He snorted happily and wriggled under her fingers.

"Obviously." Pugsley's owner sniffed. "Come along, Pugsley. There's a good boy."

Jessie watched them go, then sadly trudged back to her bench. She told herself it was for the best that the pug couldn't stay longer; she was supposed to be On The Job. She couldn't just abandon her post every time a cute dog walked by—"Aww, you have both sizes!" she called out to a blond woman walking four greyhounds, two large, two mini. She couldn't help it, she had to go see them. They were even wearing little coats.

After them, she had to visit an energetic black Lab

puppy (only six months, and just look at those paws!), then there were three corgis (who were surprisingly bossy, especially the white-and-gray one), a woman with a Chihuahua and a Great Dane (obviously, Jessie had to check out *that* combo), a couple running with some kind of husky-shepherd mix (he was a good runner, but no Angel), and an elderly man walking very slowly with a large bulldog. Jessie met them all, until—

"What do you think you're doing?"

She spun around.

Wes stood there with Pickles and Bear strapped to his waist, his scowl in full force.

"Er . . . working?" Jessie tried.

"Get back to your bench."

Jessie sighed and pet Bear on the top of his head, then crouched down to see Pickles, who wagged her little fluffy tail.

"Stop that," Wes told the dog. "She doesn't deserve your happiness."

"That's a little harsh."

"What did I tell you? Back. To. Your. Bench."

Jessie trudged back to her bench.

"And stay there," Wes called as he took his dogs past.

So Jessie stayed. And stayed. And stayed. She began to wonder if Monique was even going to come this way. Maybe she was wasting her whole life, sitting still in one place, and it was all for nothing.

And then, finally, just as that horrible thought swirled around in her head like a clump of hair caught in a bathtub drain, she saw her. The Enemy. With Sweetpea and Zelda. Jessie pulled the bill of her hat down low and held up her book to hide her face. And then she watched.

Monique came back to the park four times, each time with a different pack of dogs. She was only walking them in groups of two or, at most, three, and even then she was struggling. Jessie could see the frustration on her face as Sweetpea dug in her heels when she wanted to go in a different direction, as Ox and Marco, a pair of basset hounds, pulled her all around chasing scents, as Angel lunged at squirrels. By the time the woman was walking her last group of dogs, this time a pair of cattle dogs Jessie hadn't met before, Monique's face was drawn, her lips thin, and her movements were sharp and jerky.

"Easy money, is it?" Jessie muttered, observing how Monique trudged around the outside of the park. She didn't seem like she was having any fun at all. If Jessie and Wes made her job a little harder, would Monique give up and go away? After all, they were *just dogs* to her. She didn't love them, and she didn't love the job.

And as Jessie watched Monique clean up after one of the dogs, she had an idea for their first plan of attack. It was time for Operation Sabotage to commence.

CHAPTER 21

unrise again? Seriously, Jessie?" Ann grumbled as Jessie's alarm went off the next morning. But Jessie ignored her. It had to be sunrise. Light enough to see, dark enough to not be seen. She dressed quickly with shaking fingers, her nerves jangling around until she felt sick with them. She couldn't even eat . . .

OK, she could still eat. She grabbed a banana and a granola bar. And then another banana. And a second granola bar. Then she headed out the door, eating quickly as she half-walked, half-jogged to Wes's house. The sky was lightening around the edges, turning the houses and trees into black-and-white cutouts.

Wes opened his door at the first knock. "Time to figure out our first operation, eh?" he said.

Jessie grinned. "I already came up with one."

"You did?" He raised his eyebrows.

Jessie knew she wasn't very good at revenge, but lots of practice as a human pooper-scooper had given her a plan. She told him her idea.

Wes chuckled. "That is truly terrible. I like it."

"Really?" Jessie felt a strange mixture of pride and apprehension, like her insides were caught in a washing machine, circling over and over. "Are we . . . are we really going to do it, then?"

Wes paused, then shrugged. "You know, why not? Let's give it a try."

Wes didn't speak much on the drive to Monique's. His knuckles were white above the steering wheel and he kept shooting strange, furtive looks at Jessie. She wondered if he was having second thoughts about all of this. And sure enough, once he'd parked on the street a couple houses down, he twisted to look back at her, his expression serious. It reminded Jessie of the look her father got whenever he had to Make a Point, and she steeled herself for a lecture. "Once we start down this path, there's no turning back," he said.

"I know. And I'm ready." Jessie took a deep breath, let it out. "She took Angel from us, Wes. She took Zelda and Sweetpea and Sammy, too. Who's next?" Jessie curled her hands into fists. "She declared war first."

Wes fished Monique's key out of his glove compartment and held it in the palm of his hand as if weighing it. It wasn't heavy, but she imagined it soaking in the importance of the moment, like a sack slowly filling with grains of sand until eventually it carried the whole beach. She was almost afraid to take it from him, and when she did, it felt hot and gritty.

"You're sure?" he asked one more time.

"Yes. I want to do it." This first Operation was her idea; she wanted to be the one who carried it out.

"Be careful," he said as Jessie slipped outside, the key clenched in one sweaty fist.

She remembered all the other tips Wes had given her: walk confidently, look like you belong. Be aware of your surroundings. Calm, confident energy. Calm, confident energy. She had to repeat that to herself several times, and then she was there, she was at the car, she was unlocking it and slipping inside and closing the door.

And there were all of Monique's supplies, all unsecured and ready to be tampered with. Jessie reached toward them, then wavered. But this had to be done. For the good of Wes, and for the good of the canine nation.

"I thought this would be more exciting," Jessie said, reluctantly slicing another hole in a roll of pink, lavender-scented poop bags. It was hole number eighty-seven, in roll number five. Yes, she'd been counting. At least Wes was allowing her to sit in the front seat of his car while they worked.

"Not sure why you thought that," Wes said.

"Because it's revenge. Revenge is exciting."

Wes regarded her coolly. "You have obviously not had much experience in the art of revenge."

Jessie thought of her pathetic list of ways to get back at Loralee. Her face burned and she put another slit in the next bag. "I came up with *this* idea, didn't I?"

Wes sighed. "Yes, you did. But the truth is, most revenge is boring, tedious work. It's all about studying your enemy, setting traps, and waiting. In fact, this might be a good time for the next Rule of the Ruff."

"Really?" Jessie's hand slipped and she tore an extra-large slit in the bag. "The fifth Rule?"

Wes cleared his throat. "The fifth Rule of the Ruff is this: Be patient."

"I thought you said that wasn't a Ruff Rule, but a life rule."

"It can be both."

"But how does that apply to dogs?"

"Dogs are very patient creatures."

Jessie thought of all the dogs she'd walked and how they practically burst out of their front doors. "No, they're not."

"Are you arguing with me?"

"No."

Wes scowled. "Dogs are patient. This is not a debate."

"I wasn't debating," Jessie grumbled. "I was merely discussing."

"Well, this isn't a discussion, either. They're patient. End of story. And if you want to properly walk a dog, you have to learn to be patient, too."

Jessie rolled her eyes and poked another hole in yet another bag. She was plenty patient. Hadn't she spent an entire day on a bench? For the first time, she began to wonder if Wes was just making these Rules up as he went along.

Wes took the roll from her. "Some dogs," he said

quietly, "will sit in the same spots, staring at their front doors all day long, just waiting for their owners to show up."

"That's . . . that's really sad."

"It is." He rolled the bags up into a tight little cylinder, his large hands moving gently until the edges were all lined up. "People don't deserve that kind of devotion."

They sat in silence for a few minutes, Jessie imagining all those dogs, just sitting there, doing nothing but waiting, waiting, waiting. She shuddered. "I'm glad we're around to take them out."

Wes surprised her with a quick smile. "Me too, kid." He put the sticker back on the last bag of the roll, pinning them all together. To Jessie's eye, it looked like a brand-new roll of bags, just like all the other rolls they'd tampered with. Amazing. He pocketed them as he opened his car door. "Let's go."

"The eagle has landed," Jessie whispered into a walkie-talkie. She crouched lower, the bushes scratching at her face and neck, but she didn't care. "I repeat, the eagle has landed. Over."

"'The eagle' . . . What kind of nonsense are you spouting?" Wes's voice came through the walkie-talkie soft and crackly. It had been Jessie's idea to get walkie-talkies, because Wes, strange man that he was, didn't own a cell phone. Well, neither did she, but she wasn't an adult. She had to wait until her dad decided she was responsible enough for one. Never mind that everyone else at her school had them . . . anyways. Walkie-talkies were better. Cell phones didn't make that enjoyable crackling sound. Plus, you weren't supposed to say things like "over" or "roger that" on a cell phone.

"Explain," Wes demanded.

"I see our target. She's . . . oh. Oh no."

"What? What?"

Jessie turned down the volume on the walkie-talkie. "She's walking Sweetpea." Jessie grinned. Sweetpea always had to go to the bathroom at the start of the walk. And usually again in the middle. Sometimes a third time before the end.

"Heh. Well, keep me posted," Wes said.

"Roger that."

"And stop saying that."

"Over and out."

"That, too," Wes grumbled. The walkie-talkie crackled a few seconds longer, then went silent. Jessie turned it off, not wanting any noise to give away her position.

A sudden cry made her look up, and she gasped. Monique stood a few feet down the trail, staring at her right hand in horror. Her right hand, which was inside a poop bag. A used poop bag, but more importantly, a *ripped* poop bag.

Jessie had to smother a giggle as Monique pulled the disgusting bag off her hand, then wiped her fingers on the grass.

"Can't believe this . . . second time today." Monique used another bag to clean up her ripped bag. Unfortunately for her, that one also had a large tear in the bottom. "*Aagh!*" Monique dropped the bag with a gross *splat*. She looked at her messy hand, sighed loudly, then wiped her fingers in the grass again. Sweetpea panted happily next to her.

"Stop looking so cheerful," Monique snapped at the dog. She adjusted the leash in her left hand, then continued walking, her right hand held out a foot in front of her body so it wouldn't contaminate the rest of her.

"Hey! Hey, ma'am! You left your doggie bag," a man called after her. Monique's shoulders stiffened, but she kept walking, leaving the ripped bags behind. "Hey! They're not going to clean themselves up, you know!" Monique walked faster, turning a corner and hurrying off the main trail. "Can you believe that?" the man said to a woman walking a small terrier. "Just left those bags there."

"I know. So rude," the woman agreed. "It's people like *that* who get dogs banned from places." She patted her own stash of doggie bags, clearly wanting to show she wasn't a person like *that*.

"I've seen her here before," the man mused. "I think she's a dog walker."

"Well. Clearly not a very good one." The woman lifted her nose in the air and continued walking down the trail, and moments later, the man resumed his jog. Neither of them bothered to clean up the abandoned bags themselves.

Jessie waited a few minutes longer, then ducked out of the bushes when she was sure no one was around. She used a large stick to pick up the bags and carry them to the garbage bin down the trail. Then she turned on her walkie-talkie. "First mission a success," she said.

Crackle. Crackle. "No 'roger' this time?" Wes's voice came through the static.

"It would be 'over,' not 'roger,'" Jessie sighed.

"You OK, kiddo? Not having second thoughts, are you?"

"Of course not." Monique deserved this. She deserved worse than this. If Monique wanted "easy money," she should do something else. Dog walking was an art.

"OK then. Meet me back by my car." He hesitated, then begrudgingly added, "Wes, over and out."

That brought a smile to Jessie's lips. "Over and out," she said.

"Someone looks determined," Wes said as Jessie joined him by his car. "Eye of the tiger."

"Eye of the dog," Jessie corrected solemnly.

Wes chuckled. He seemed much more relaxed now that they had begun Operation Sabotage, his sadness from last week practically forgotten. Yet more proof that they were doing the right thing. *She* was doing the right thing.

"Wes?"

Wes turned. A woman got out of her car and waved to him. She had reddish-blond hair clipped back in a low ponytail, and there was something vaguely familiar about her . . .

"*Howoo?*" A little wolfy dog Jessie knew all too well hopped out of the car and trotted up to Wes. "*Howooo*," she sang. Wes leaned down and pet her head.

Hazel and Hazel's owner. Clearly.

"I'm glad I caught you. I was wondering if you'd like to do lunch?" the woman asked.

Wes hesitated.

"I mean, only if you want to," she added quickly. "I know you're usually busy."

Wes glanced at Jessie, then back at the woman. "Why not?"

"Really?" Her whole face brightened. It was like watching a dog about to be leashed for a walk.

"Absolutely." Wes turned to Jessie. "Think you can handle the afternoon pack? Pickles, Bear, and Presto?"

Jessie froze. "Me?"

"No, my other assistant. And before you ask, no, I don't actually have another assistant."

"I know that," Jessie grumbled. Her heart beat faster. Could she handle the whole dog walk on her own? Just her and the dogs? "I can take them," she decided.

Wes grinned and clapped her on the shoulder. "You've got this, kid." And then he got into the front seat of the woman's car, Hazel leaping onto his lap. The woman gave Jessie one last quizzical look, got back in her car, and drove off.

And Jessie was on her own. A dog walker, flying solo. She took a deep breath and set out. It was going to take a lot longer without a car, but that didn't matter. She had her feet, and she had her hip pack, and she was ready.

CHAPTER 22

J essie ate her dinner that night without complaint, even though it was a tuna casserole and her aunt always put onions in it.

It had been an exhausting afternoon walking those dogs by herself and running to each house in between. Exhausting, but fun, and she was feeling pretty proud of herself. But now it was time to get back to Operation Sabotage: She needed to figure out their next move.

She helped clear the table without being asked, and as she put away the leftovers, she glanced around the fridge for something . . . anything . . .

There. Wrapped in parchment paper and thawing on the top shelf was their customary Thursday night fish.

Jessie reached for it.

"I'm surprised by you, Jessie," Aunt Beatrice said behind her.

Jessie jumped and slammed the fridge shut, her heart in her throat, the fish in her hand. She turned, keeping her hands behind her back. "S-surprised?" she managed, guilt blazing across her face. Did her aunt know what she was planning?

"You've been doing more chores lately without waiting to be told. It shows a new level of maturity for you." Aunt Beatrice beamed. "I'll have to mention it to your dad."

"Th-thanks," Jessie said, her mouth thick. After her aunt left the kitchen, Jessie stood there for a long moment, the stolen fish heavy in her hands. Her aunt had never smiled at her like that before. Not once.

She opened the fridge and started to put the fish back, then stopped. An image popped into her head: that sideways look Loralee had given her last summer when she invited Ann to come with her. A look that told Jessie *You don't matter.* A smug, triumphant look. *You want to come walk with me? That is, unless you're busy.* Loralee had known what Ann's response would be. No one was too busy for *her.* Even Max. He'd turned Loralee down once to stay with Jessie, but a few days later, Jessie had lost him, too.

Just like Wes had lost Sweetpea. And Zelda. And Angel. Jessie remembered the condescending way Monique had bragged about it in the car. *The people around here are practically begging me to take their dogs out. At this rate, Wes will be folding up his business in no time.* She thought she'd already won, too.

Jessie closed the fridge door. She couldn't back out now. Her aunt might not understand, but she was doing this for Wes. And for the dogs.

Before Jessie could chicken out, she stuffed the fish

inside a gallon ziplock bag, tucked the bag under her shirt, and snuck through the house.

Ann was on the phone when Jessie slipped into their room.

"Uh-huh. Yeah, that really sucks. Uh-huh. Sounds like he's just being a jerk. Definitely." Ann glanced up at Jessie. She stuck out her tongue and rolled her eyes. "Hey, I've gotta run. Maybe this weekend? Yes? Yeah, Saturday would be great! OK." She hung up, then tossed her phone to the side.

"What's up in Loralee land?" Jessie asked.

"Oh, I guess Max is being weird. He said she can't come to dinner with them Friday night."

"Dinner?" A sudden suspicion hit Jessie harder than a charging dog. "Dinner *here*?"

"Yes, here. Didn't Mom tell you?"

Jessie shook her head.

"Well, they're coming over at six P.M. on Friday. And before you get any ideas, I don't think there are enough chores in the world to save you if Mom catches you trying to sneak away again."

"I wasn't even considering it," Jessie grumbled. And she hadn't been. OK, maybe just a little, just for a second. "So . . . Max told Loralee she couldn't come with them?" Did that mean he wanted to see her without Loralee around? That thought made her feel strange, like her heart couldn't decide if it wanted to beat harder or stop beating altogether.

"Sounds like it." Ann blew her bangs off her forehead and smiled. "Maybe this'll be your chance to make your big move."

"My big—oh. Shut up, Ann." Jessie scowled.

"I have some clothes you could borrow. You know, if you wanted to dress a little . . . differently."

Jessie glanced down at her T-shirt and shorts. They looked just fine to her. Then she studied Ann's outfit, the way her teal shirt clung to her and brought out the color in her eyes, how her legs looked longer somehow in the cut of her jeans. She shook her head. Ann's clothing looked tight and uncomfortable. She didn't want to dress like that. Did she?

"Or not." Ann shrugged and picked up a magazine. "Let me know if you change your mind."

"Don't hold your breath," Jessie muttered. She had to stay focused. "I have an errand to run. Will you cover for me?"

Ann frowned. "Where are you going?"

"Just . . . just another mission. You know, for the dog-walking thing."

"At eight at night?"

"It has to be at night." It was still light out now, but it would be dark soon. Dark was what she needed.

"Does this have something to do with that badly hidden lump under your shirt?"

"What lump?" Jessie asked.

Ann rolled her eyes.

"Fine," Jessie said. "It may, or may not, have something to do with this alleged lump."

Ann shook her head. "You're ridiculous, Jessie. But just . . . be careful."

"I'll be careful," Jessie promised. She opened the

window, popped off the screen, and slipped out into the cool evening air, bringing the ziplock of fish with her. Then she remembered something. "Hey, Ann?" She poked her head back up.

"Did you see reason?" Ann asked. "Change your mind?"

"Who do you think you're talking to?" Jessie scoffed.

Ann sighed. "What, then?"

"Can I borrow one of your bikes?" Jessie grinned. Two minutes later, she was racing through the night, the wheels of Ann's spare bike whirring softly beneath her.

The next morning, Jessie was practically bursting as she waited for Wes on his doorstep. And waited. He was late. It was full-on morning by now, the sky bright and turning blue as the sun rose lazily into view. She knocked on his door again and again until, finally, he opened it.

"What do you want?" he demanded, then sighed. "Never mind. Don't answer that. Just . . . just give me a few minutes to finish my coffee, and I'll be right out." He shut the door so quickly she couldn't even manage her foot save.

Jessie paced back and forth. Something about his words bothered her. Why wasn't he drinking on the porch? He always drank his coffee on the porch. He . . .

Wait a second. He didn't drink coffee! He always drank *tea*! What was going on?

Wes came outside. He looked . . . different somehow.

"What?" he asked. "Why are you staring at me?"

"Did you brush your hair?"

"Maybe."

Jessie narrowed her eyes. "Why? You never brush your hair. You told me the dogs don't care what you look like."

"Well, maybe I thought I'd make an effort anyhow." Wes scowled, running a hand self-consciously through his long grayish-blond hair.

"And why are you drinking coffee?" Jessie demanded. "I thought you said it was a crutch."

Wes's furrow deepened. "Do you want to stand here and ask useless questions, or do you want to get going?" He didn't wait for an answer as he headed to his car.

Jessie glanced once more at his closed front door and then followed him. She felt unsettled, like she was wearing two different kinds of shoes. Wes had always seemed like the kind of person who would never change. She didn't like that he was suddenly taking his appearance seriously and drinking coffee. She didn't like it at all.

Wes settled in the front seat of the car and waited until she climbed in back and clipped in her seat belt before saying, "I thought we would start with—"

"Angel," Jessie said quickly. "We need to drive to Angel's house." All thoughts of Wes's weird behaviors vanished as Jessie told him her plan. The one she had already implemented.

"So you want to keep doing this," he said.

Jessie frowned. Was that a hint of reluctance? "Has Monique quit the biz yet?" she demanded.

"Doubtful."

"Then yes, I want to keep doing this." Jessie crossed her arms.

Wes's lips twitched upward. "OK then."

A few minutes later, he pulled in behind a large gray van. "This work?"

Jessie looked out the window. They had a perfect view of Angel's house. She nodded, then settled back in her seat to watch. Would this be the thing to break Monique, to send her out of the business and out of Wes's way?

She thought of Max suddenly. Max, who she hadn't seen since that disastrous party last week, when he'd been kissing Loralee right in front of her. Max, who had told Loralee she couldn't come to dinner Friday night . . . Jessie put her hands against her face. Her skin felt too hot. She didn't care if Max moved away and she didn't see him ever again. It didn't matter to her.

She had to stop thinking about him.

Jessie glanced at Wes. He was obviously lost in his own thoughts, his lips curved up in a smile. Weird. "Hey." She nudged his shoulder. "You haven't asked me how the afternoon dog walks went."

"That's because I have the utmost faith in your abilities."

"Really?" Pride filled Jessie's chest until she thought she might burst with it, like an overinflated balloon.

"Of course. You were trained by the best."

Jessie deflated a little. "So really, you have the utmost faith in your own abilities."

"Exactly."

"Fine then, I'm not going to ask you how your date went."

Wes's smile vanished. "It wasn't a date."

Jessie blinked. "But, you went to lunch with Hazel's mom. It sure *looked* like a date."

"It was merely lunch with an old friend. I don't date. Not anymore."

"But—"

"Oh look, our target is approaching."

Jessie shook her head but dropped the subject as Monique parked in front of Angel's house and went inside the gate. A few minutes later Angel was pulling her straight to the car. Monique opened the door to the back, and Angel dove in . . . and then started barking like mad, jumping around, leaping into the front, then the back.

"Angel, stop! Angel, in back!" Monique tried to get the pit bull under control, but Angel was a dog on a mission and he wasn't stopping for anything.

The front door opened. "What the heck is going on out here?" Bill, the owner, demanded.

"Oh, uh, he's just a little extra excited today," Monique said, as behind her Angel attempted to rip apart the seat. "Angel! Stop that!"

"Are you sure you can handle him?" Bill's shoulders hunched up so high Jessie thought they might wrap right around his head.

"Of course I can. I'll just . . . I'll be off now." Monique got in and shut her door, and Jessie watched her drive off, Angel still jumping all around the back seat. Jessie glanced back at Bill. He was watching the car, too, and he didn't look happy. Not happy at all.

"I'd call that a success. I just hope the rest of her dogs are as difficult." Wes grinned. "Good job, apprentice. You've really taken to the art of sabotage."

Jessie wanted to feel proud, but somehow his words felt more like an insult.

The following day, Wes gave her the morning off from dog walking and had her meet him at noon on the far end of the park. Thanks to Jessie's spying, they knew Monique always took a midday reading break on a bench in the middle of the park, leaving her car unattended.

"I figured it was my turn to come up with something," Wes explained. He leaned casually against a nearby tree, a yellow towel slung over his shoulder and a bucket at his feet. The bucket was full of a congealing liquid that smelled strongly of bacon.

Jessie shook her head. "I'm not sure we should do that."

"What?"

"Whatever it is you have planned with that, that . . . what is that, anyways?"

"This?" Wes lifted the bucket. "It's bacon grease."

Jessie wrinkled her nose. "It's disgusting."

"Are you a vegetarian?"

"I might be now," she muttered, as another waft of the smell hit her. The heat of the day baking around them certainly didn't help, either.

Wes grinned. "Well, your plan yesterday and the day before got me thinking. I was a little skeptical initially, but I've decided that maybe you're on the right track."

"You really think so?"

"Absolutely," Wes said. "If all we have to do is make things a little more challenging for our competition, then I'm all in." He tossed Jessie the key. "Leashes," he ordered.

Jessie glanced around, then unlocked the car and pulled out the tangle of leashes. Grimacing, she dunked each of them into the bucket of grease, trying to ignore the pieces of fat, the way the liquid sloshed around, all oily and awful. She was never eating bacon again. Probably.

"Now pat them dry, but gently." Wes handed her the towel. "And quickly."

"You could help, you know," Jessie grumbled as she patted each leash, trying to soak up the extra fluid. "After all, this one was *your* idea."

"I *am* helping. I'm supervising."

Shaking her head, Jessie finished with the leashes, dropped them back in the car, and locked up.

Whistling, Wes picked up the bucket and headed down the trail with Jessie at his heels. "The first half of Operation Three is complete. Ready for the second half?"

"We're doing more today?" Jessie glanced over her shoulder, but no one was watching. "Don't you have your own dogs to walk?"

Wes's good mood evaporated. "No, actually. I don't have any dog walks this afternoon." Silence thickened around them until Jessie felt like she was swimming through that bucket of bacon grease.

"Er, what's the second half?" she finally asked, unable to take it any longer.

"I thought you'd never ask." His grin was back in place, but it looked fake, as if he'd remembered to pull his lips back but forgot to tell the rest of his face that he was smiling. Jessie had to look away, and she didn't complain, not even when he told her the plan. Not even when he told her what she'd have to do. And not even when he handed her the horrifying bucket.

"Zelda, stop! Stop, you, you muppet!" Monique's voice was loud and shrill, easily carrying over the sound of barking. "Ack! Sweetpea, no! Why are you doing this? No, no, Sammy, not you, too!"

Jessie peeked out from behind her tree. Monique was struggling to walk three dogs down the main path. Each dog was very intent on jumping at the leashes of the others. So intent they didn't seem to care if they crashed into each other, or into Monique.

"I say, can't you control your dogs?" a passerby said.

"This is ridiculous," another person declared. A third person took a quick picture as Monique flushed and pleaded with the dogs, eventually getting them into some sort of order.

Jessie chewed her lip. Monique looked like she was on the verge of tears, and it made Jessie's chest feel tight. She knew exactly what that felt like, how hard it was to keep moving when your eyesight was all blurry, and you couldn't blink or the tears would tumble down your cheeks and everyone would see you were crying. Did Monique really deserve this?

The people around here are practically begging me to take their dogs out. Wes will be folding up his business in no time.

Jessie recalled Monique's words, and her hands clenched around the handle of the bucket. She squashed the guilty part of herself down, picturing it as a piece of paper to be crushed into a tiny, tiny ball. She had to stay strong. Monique could always quit and do something else, something that wouldn't ruin Wes's life and take away the one thing he cared about.

Jessie headed further into the park, along the route she knew Monique would take, spilling bacon grease along the way until the bucket was empty. As she jogged back through the park, she could hear the dogs barking, could hear the desperation in Monique's voice. She reminded herself again that Monique deserved this, and she tried not to listen to the sounds of chaos behind her. She imagined herself once more as a spy. Just a spy following orders.

CHAPTER 23

Mom is on a rampage," Ann said the moment Jessie walked in the door. "I guess our Thursday night fish has gone missing?"

Jessie froze, her heart in her mouth. She could taste its pulse beating in her throat. It tasted like blood and panic, smothered in guilt. The image of her aunt smiling proudly filled her head, and her stomach twisted like one of Monique's leashes.

"Stop looking like that," Ann said. "It's not that big a deal. Dad said he'd take us all out to Bantavi's for dinner. He thinks maybe he just forgot to buy the fish this week." Ann shrugged. "If you can stop making that face and keep your mouth shut, we'll all be eating ravioli and this whole thing will blow right over."

Jessie swallowed, then nodded. She tried to smooth out her expression, picturing her face as a mask, blank and lifeless.

"Now you just look constipated," Ann said.

Jessie scowled at her.

"That's better." Ann laughed.

"Ah, Jessie. Glad you're here," Uncle David said breezily. "We're heading out for dinner tonight."

"Ask her about the fish," Aunt Beatrice called from the kitchen.

"For the last time, Bea, forget about the fish!" Uncle David yelled. "Let's just go, have a nice family dinner, and move on, OK?"

Jessie got ready quickly and quietly, then spent the whole drive into town looking out the window, trying to avoid eye contact with anyone.

"Stop looking so twitchy," Ann hissed as they trailed her parents into the restaurant. "It just screams guilty conscience."

"I'm not being . . ." Jessie's jaw dropped, the words falling right out of her mouth.

"What? What are you looking at?" Ann spun, searching the room, and then she saw him, too. "Oh my," she whispered.

Sitting in the corner, looking strange in a button-down shirt with barely any dog hair clinging to it, was Wes. And he wasn't alone, either. At first Jessie thought he was out on another one of those nondate dates with Hazel's owner. But as they followed the hostess past his table, she got a better look at the woman, and she realized she wasn't Hazel's owner. Still, she *did* look familiar. A sudden image came to mind, an image of a woman leaning against Wes with a leash wrapped around her wrist, a woman with long, frizzy, blond hair.

Was that . . . Wes's ex-wife?

"Stop staring," Ann hissed.

But Jessie couldn't help it. Was this why Wes seemed happier recently? But he didn't look happy now. He looked . . . like her dad, she realized. Like her dad whenever they went out to dinner with his friends. Like part of him was sitting there and laughing with them, but the rest of him was endlessly searching the space between the seats, waiting for Jessie's mom to come back and knowing she never would.

Jessie finally tore her eyes away from Wes, and when the waiter came for her order, she found herself ordering the fish, even though she was tired of it, even though this was her chance for something different.

She wanted to pretend things didn't always change.

Beep-beep! Beep-beep!

"Turn it off, would you?" Ann threw a pillow at Jessie. "It's been going off for, like, five minutes already."

"Sorry, didn't hear it," Jessie mumbled, hitting the off switch on her alarm. She hadn't slept well, and she felt like her head was stuffed full of cloth. Still, it was Friday. Just today and she could take the weekend off. She loved walking the dogs, but these sabotage missions were taking their toll on her.

"You're the worst," Ann grumbled. "These sunrise excursions have got to end. Seriously."

"Duly noted." Jessie got dressed quickly and was out before Ann could yell at her any more.

She found Wes outside his house with his mug of tea. She'd planned on asking him about his date, but he actually looked happy to see her for once, and she didn't want to ruin that.

"I have good news, kiddo," he said.

"Should I be worried?"

"Very funny." He took a sip. "Zelda is back."

"Really?"

He nodded. "Apparently her people heard how much trouble the other dog walker was having with her. No amount of pictures and cute notes could smooth it over." He chuckled.

"That's . . . that's great," Jessie said.

"It gets better. Sweetpea is back, too. Her people decided they didn't want someone so irresponsible to be walking her. Something about leaving bags of poop on the trail?" His grin was so wide Jessie felt sure his face would split.

Jessie tried on her own smile. She wasn't sure why, but it felt unnatural, like forcing a glove over a foot. "So, does that mean we won? We can stop Operation Sabotage?" Maybe she just wasn't cut out for this life of crime.

"No, kiddo, this is just the beginning."

Jessie's heart sank. "Oh."

Wes carefully placed his mug on the coaster on the top porch step and stood up, streaks of light slowly lengthening across the sky behind him.

"Do I at least get another Rule of the Ruff?" Jessie asked. "Something like 'It's a dog-eat-dog world'?"

He winced. "That is a particularly offensive expression. And no. No new Rules today. Instead, I have something else planned." He led her around to his backyard, where he picked up . . .

"Not another bucket," Jessie groaned.

"Don't worry, this one just smells like paint."

"Why?"

"Because it *is* paint."

"Oh." A few seconds later, she had to ask. "Er, why are we bringing a bucket full of paint?"

Wes grinned. "You'll see."

Jessie felt like she'd created a monster. Like her first pranks had just opened the door for Wes's inner child to come roaring out, and now there was no shutting it back in until he was done. Just like when she'd run with Angel, all she could do was hang on and see it through.

Crackle-crackle. "Done yet, kiddo?" *Hiss-crackle.*

"Roger that." Jessie carefully folded the towels and put them back on Monique's front seat. Then she locked the door and slipped away with the bucket of remaining paint, not stopping until she reached a large elm tree. Hiding the bucket, she sat down and waited. She didn't have to wait long.

". . . believe you two, jumping into the pond like that," Monique was saying. She had a pair of very bedraggled white poodles with her. "Honestly. Why do you always do that?"

The dogs looked at her, their dripping faces unapologetic. Jessie shrank down farther as Monique unlocked her car and grabbed one of her green towels.

"What the—oh no. No. How? How is this happening?" Monique's voice dropped to a low mutter as she wiped frantically at the dog's fur, which was turning more and more green.

Jessie stood up and quietly crept away, holding back her laughter. At least this was harmless. Wes had assured her the paint was completely nontoxic, so it would just wash out and wouldn't be a big deal—

"What have you done to my dogs?"

Jessie stopped and turned back. A very tall, thin man was yelling at Monique, his voice cutting across the quiet of the park until everyone was watching. "Look at them! Just look at their beautiful fur. Once so white, so fluffy . . . and now this!"

"I-I'm sorry. The towel, maybe the dye from the towel is—"

The man didn't let Monique finish. He just grabbed his dogs away from her and marched off.

"He's an eccentric, that one," Wes said, suddenly next to Jessie. She jumped, almost falling over. "Sorry, kiddo, didn't mean to scare you. Good work, eh?"

"H-how did he know to come here?"

Wes looked innocently at his fingernails. "Someone may have left him an anonymous message that his dogs were in trouble." He dropped the act. "Luke and Leia are show dogs, or they used to be when they were younger. He takes their grooming extremely seriously." He started walking and Jessie hurried to fall into step beside him. She wanted to be as far from the scene of the crime as she could be. Even though the yelling hadn't been directed at her, she could feel the man's anger like it was burrowing into her skin.

"Your turn, kiddo. What's our next Operation?"

Jessie shrugged. That little ball of guilt deep inside her was beginning to unfold.

Wes stopped suddenly and looked at her, *really* looked at her. "Did you want to take a break?"

She nodded.

His grin faded. "All right, kid. We gave her a tough week. We can ease up for a bit and see what happens."

"Thank you." Jessie dug around in her pocket and pulled out Monique's key. "For safekeeping," she said, handing it to Wes. She didn't want to carry it anymore. It felt like it was burning her.

CHAPTER 24

Showered, presentable, and present," Jessie recited. "Check, check, and check."

"Are you sure about that shirt?" Ann asked.

"Yes, I'm sure. Quit bugging me." Jessie tugged at her navy blue college basketball team T-shirt. It was one of her favorites, even if it wasn't soccer.

"No time to change it now; they should be here any minute," Aunt Beatrice said, setting a platter in the middle of the table.

"Why would I change it?"

"Change what?" Uncle David asked as he wandered into the kitchen. "Don't ever change a thing, Jessie."

"Don't worry, Dad. Jessie never changes." Ann shook her head and finished setting the silverware on the table.

"What's gotten into you?" Jessie whispered to her cousin.

Ann pursed her lips but didn't say anything.

Fine, Jessie thought. *Whatever.* Ann had been acting a little nicer lately, but clearly she was back to Ann-Marie again.

The doorbell rang.

"Coming," Aunt Beatrice trilled. Jessie's stomach did a flip-flop. She felt like she was on top of a roller coaster, about to plummet down, only the tracks were missing. She didn't want to sit with Monique. She didn't want to play nice and eat dinner with the woman who was stealing her dogs.

And then she looked up, and her eyes met Max's as he walked into the kitchen. He didn't even seem like the same Max, in his button-down plaid shirt and khaki shorts and missing his trademark hat. He looked away from her quickly, and her face heated. Was he . . . was he mad at her? Was *she* mad at *him*? Her stomach was so full of conflicting emotions, she wasn't sure she'd be able to eat. Luckily it was meatloaf today, so that would be no big loss.

"It smells wonderful, Bea. Thanks for having us." Monique smiled warmly. "And I see we have the elusive Jessie here."

"H-hi." Jessie swallowed. If looking at Max was hard, looking at Monique was like trying to stare at the sun, a sun you'd been actively sabotaging the whole week. She could feel the guilt blazing across her face like a neon sign.

"Well now, isn't this nice?" Aunt Beatrice beamed. "Go ahead and sit. I made meatloaf."

"Aren't we lucky," Jessie muttered under her breath. Max heard her, his lips quirking up, but he still didn't look at her as he took a seat next to his mother.

Ann tried to nudge Jessie over to the seat next to

Max, but Jessie ignored her, and finally her cousin sighed loudly and took that chair instead.

"You're being stupid," Ann whispered.

"So's your face," Jessie whispered back.

Ann rolled her eyes and muttered something about "childish" and "missed opportunities." Definitely back to Ann-Marie.

There was a lot of polite small talk at the table that Jessie easily ignored as she poked at her food, conscious the whole time of Max, of where he was sitting, of how he was eating. Even though she didn't look at him, not once. OK, maybe once. Or twice, but very briefly. And even though he didn't say anything, she was very aware of his silence. What was wrong with her?

Even worse, the whole time she kept waiting for Monique to mention dogs or Wes. As the conversation droned on and on and it didn't happen, Jessie imagined herself as a spring being tightened and tightened, until her insides were so twisted she wasn't sure if it was anxiety or the taste of meatloaf that was making her nauseous.

But, of course, Ann couldn't let sleeping dogs lie. "Is it true your sister walks dogs for Bianca?" she burst out.

"Ann-Marie, I told you not to pester her about that," Aunt Bea said quickly, but Jessie noticed how she leaned forward eagerly, like she was dying to hear more about this, too. Why was everyone so interested in this Bianca person? All she did was sing. Jessie didn't get it.

"Oh yes. Grace is a 'celebrity dog walker.'" Monique made those annoying air quotes next to her head. "She's the one who convinced me to get into the dog-walking biz."

"It's probably not as glamorous here as it is in Hollywood," Aunt Beatrice said.

Monique winced. Was she thinking about the ripped poop bags? The bacon juice on her leashes? Jessie couldn't bear to watch, so she poked at her food as talk of celebrities and Hollywood washed over her, leaving her safely untouched.

"You know, Jessie's been getting into the dog-walking business, too," Uncle David said.

Jessie froze, her fork stuck in her half-eaten meatloaf. She'd really been hoping that wouldn't come up.

"Is that so?" Monique's voice was surprised, but her eyes were not. They had the same kind of look in them that Jessie had seen in her dad's eyes when he was about to haggle for something he wanted.

"Yeah, she's been working with ole Wes down the street," Uncle David blabbed. "Isn't that right, Jessie?"

Jessie yanked her fork out of her meatloaf. There was no way she'd be able to eat it now. Not with Monique staring at her like that. *Stop looking at me, please*, Jessie thought at her. *Just leave me alone.* She suddenly felt the strangest urge to confess all her crimes. *Yes, I cut holes in your doggie bags. I put fish in your car. It was me!* She had to clamp her lips closed to keep those words squashed down inside. She pictured herself as a garbage disposal, smashing all her lies and guilt and sabotage down and down and down.

"Jessie, you want to tell Monique about dog walking?" Aunt Beatrice chimed in. "You could compare notes."

That was the last thing Jessie wanted to do. She thought of her dad again and tried one of his expressions instead. "Let's talk about something else. I don't like to mix business with pleasure."

Monique's eyes widened, and this time the surprise in them was genuine. She burst out laughing.

"Jessie," Aunt Bea began warningly, but Monique waved her off.

"It's fine, Bea," Monique said, launching into another story about her sister's Hollywood life.

Jessie relaxed. Still, she caught Monique glancing at her throughout the rest of the meal and knew it wasn't over yet.

After dinner, Aunt Beatrice made Jessie and Ann clear the table and start on the dishes while she headed out to the porch with Monique. "Max can help, too," Monique said, giving her son a meaningful look.

"Nonsense. He's a guest," Aunt Beatrice protested.

"I'm a guest, too," Jessie said, but at her aunt's dark look, she shut her mouth and grabbed a stack of plates. Max followed her, his hands full of silverware.

"I just remembered, I have to be somewhere else," Ann said, leaving Jessie alone in the kitchen with Max.

Jessie shifted uncomfortably, stepping way to the side so Max would have plenty of room to dump the silverware in the sink. "You really don't have to help," she said as he turned on the water. "Honest."

Max shrugged. "Might as well be useful." He glanced sideways at her. "Why are you being so weird?"

"Me? I'm being the normal amount of weird. Why are you being so weird?"

"The normal amount of weird?" He grinned. "I didn't realize there was such a thing."

"It's carefully calibrated." She inched a little closer and picked up the sponge.

"No dishwasher?"

"You're looking at her." Jessie scrubbed half-heartedly at a plate. Meatloaf was the worst to clean off. It looked a little too much like the piles she was stuck cleaning up for Wes.

That made her think of Monique and the ripped bags, and she flushed.

"Seriously, though, you OK?" Max asked.

"Never better." She half-turned from him.

"If that's the face of never better, then we're all in trouble." He turned the hot water on top of his pile of silverware and then liberally squirted soap over all of them. "I notice you haven't been back to the park to play soccer in a while."

"I haven't really had time." Last time she'd played Max, Loralee had come by and thrown her little fit, and Max had been quick to ditch Jessie. She wasn't about to put herself through that again.

"Well, maybe once we're done here, we should do something fun." Again with the sideways look. It seemed out of place on him, like a dog walking upright. "Like . . . we could go for ice cream?"

"Tonight?" Jessie asked.

"Sure, why not? My mom would drive us. She suggested it, actually."

"She did?"

"She thought you might like to . . . to get away a little, after dinner."

"Oh." Jessie didn't know what to think of that. "Wouldn't . . . wouldn't that make Loralee angry? I mean, she didn't even like you playing soccer with me."

Max frowned. "I'm *not* always glued to her side, OK? I'm free to eat ice cream with anyone I want."

"Max! You ready?" Monique called from the front of the house.

Max shut off the water and looked at Jessie. "You coming?"

"You call that done?" Jessie picked up a fork. It still had food stuck to it. Gross.

He shrugged. "Done enough."

"That was the worst washing job I've ever seen."

"You want to stay here and rewash the dishes or go eat ice cream?"

Moments later, Jessie was out the door, following Max and his mother. "You sure you don't want to go?" she asked Ann.

"I'm sure. You go and have fun with Max." Ann gave Jessie a sly smile, which vanished when Jessie told her the dishes weren't done yet.

"Kids in back," Monique said, sounding a tiny bit like Wes.

Jessie got into the back seat next to Max and pulled on her seat belt. Monique started the car and the doors automatically locked.

Jessie's mouth went dry. She'd just gotten into a car . . .

with the *enemy*. She was trapped, right here at the scene of so many of her crimes. What had she been thinking? How could she let the promise of ice cream with Max take over her better judgment?

Jessie's stomach twisted, and not just because of the faint smell of rotting fish. She could feel Monique watching her in the rearview mirror. She could feel it, and she was powerless to stop whatever was coming.

CHAPTER 25

At first Monique didn't say anything at all. She just drove, like she was a normal mom taking kids to get ice cream, and not like a merciless dog stealer who'd caught herself an enemy spy. Jessie wasn't fooled, though, and she desperately tried to remember the Rules of the Ruff, hoping one of them could help her.

Calm, confident energy . . . impossible right now. OK, be aware of your surroundings. Jessie glanced around as they headed down the street. She could do that. Know when to leave it. Well, she still thought that rule was useless, and it certainly didn't help her here. Always be ready. She swallowed, not sure what she'd be ready for. A surprise attack? Monique torturing her for information? And finally, be patient.

Patient.

Jessie took a deep breath, let it out slowly. She would wait, then. Wait and see what Monique was up to.

"You doing OK there, Jessie?" Monique glanced at her in the rearview mirror. "The dog fur isn't bothering you, is it?"

"No, I'm used to it." Whoops! Jessie clamped her mouth shut before any more information could slip out. The last thing she wanted was to talk about her familiarity with all things dog.

Monique's laugh was warm and rich. "I guess you would be, after working with Wes." Another look in the mirror.

Jessie gulped. The air felt charged now, like a thunderstorm was brewing. Here it was.

"Beatrice mentioned you might be getting a dog at the end of the summer?" Monique said.

Jessie blinked. That was *not* the question she'd been expecting. "I-I hope so."

"You know I wanted a dog when I was younger, too."

Max groaned. "Mom, please, not the dog story again."

"My mom promised me and my sister we could get a dog," Monique continued, ignoring her son, "but we'd have to be responsible for everything. It was a lot more work than I thought it would be. I couldn't hang out with my friends after school if it was my turn to take Sadie out. Or this one time, I saved up for months to go on a trip to New York, but then Sadie ate a sock and needed surgery. So, trip canceled." Monique's laugh was pained, as if this long-ago trip that never happened still bothered her. "Nowadays, I like borrowing dogs much better than having one around all the time."

Jessie felt the first faint squiggles of unease in her stomach. She had soccer practices later this year. Would a dog get in the way of that? Which would she choose? The dog, definitely. Right? But what if her dog got sick, too? Could her dad afford the vet bills? Monique stared at her through the rearview mirror like she was waiting for an answer, so Jessie said, "I know that dogs are a lot of responsibility."

"You'll probably be just fine, then," Monique said. "You seem very responsible; I've seen you out working with Wes. Looks like he's got you working hard."

"He tries." Jessie fiddled with the edge of her T-shirt. Next to her, Max turned so he was pointedly looking out the window, as if he wanted nothing to do with this conversation. Jessie wished she could do the same.

"So . . . how's business?" Monique pulled up to the ice-cream parlor. "You know, for Wes?"

Jessie stiffened. Of *course*, this was what Monique wanted to know. "Good. Business is good."

Monique's eyes widened. "I didn't mean to pry—"

Jessie yanked open her door, grateful the parlor was so close. "Thanks for the ride," she said, firm but polite. Her dad would have been proud.

Monique nodded. "You're . . . you're welcome." Max opened his door and started to get out. "Max, wait. A word, please?"

He grimaced and shut his door. Jessie got out and closed her door, then leaned her back against it. The sun was just sinking below the horizon, leaving behind streaks of fire. It still felt warm, too, the heat of the day radiating around her, then slowly draining away into the chill of night. She closed her eyes and enjoyed it. She'd survived. Her first interrogation, and she'd made it through. And now, now she was getting ice cream . . . with Max. Almost like a date. Her treacherous heart leapt like an unleashed dog, even though she knew it wasn't a date at all. He was still with Loralee.

The door next to her opened and Max practically sprang out. "No need to wait, we'll walk back," he told his mother, then slammed the door. "Let's go." Without waiting to see if Jessie would follow, he stalked toward the parlor.

Jessie frowned, not sure at this sudden change. Was it something she'd done? Maybe he didn't want to be here with her? She slowly headed into the Ice Cream Scream. The air-conditioning slammed into her, but it did nothing to cool the heat rising in her face. Even the ghost mascot didn't make her smile.

Max waited by the counter, his shoulders tense. He glanced at Jessie, then away again. "So. What kind you want?"

"What's it to you?"

"What's it—wha?" He scrunched up his face. "I . . . don't understand."

"Well, you seem angry, so I figured we were fighting. I was just going along."

He grinned suddenly, his sharp canines on full display. "You are such a weirdo. Thanks."

"You're welcome?" She wasn't sure if it was a compliment or an insult, but just seeing him smile like that, with his dimples and the way his nose crinkled . . . she shook herself. What was wrong with her? She was being ridiculous. "Everything OK?" she asked.

"Yeah. My mom just wants me to do something,

and I don't want to. But it's fine. Some might say 'never better.'" His grin widened. "And for the record, this is a much better face for 'never better.'" He pointed at his smile.

"That looks like a face for selling used cars."

"Ouch."

"Also chocolate."

"What?"

"My ice-cream flavor. Chocolate. Unless there's chocolate fudge brownie?"

"There most certainly is!" The teenager behind the counter sounded a little too enthusiastic, like he was very eager to get rid of it.

"Er . . . maybe just chocolate, after all," Jessie mumbled.

"So, your own dog, huh? That's your endgame?" Max asked. They had finished their ice cream a while ago and were taking their time walking back to Ann's house.

Jessie felt relaxed and happy for the first time in days. It was dark out, but not full dark, the sky hanging on to tendrils of light. All up and down the road, streetlights filled the rest of the night with little pockets of brightness, and she was walking next to Max with no Loralee in sight. Not a bad way to end a Friday.

"Do you know what kind you'll get?" he asked.

"I haven't decided yet. But lately . . . I've been thinking I kind of want a Klee Kai."

"A what what?"

She laughed. "It looks like a husky, only small, like twenty pounds."

"That sounds like the cutest dog ever."

"Yeah, that's what everyone says. The one I know, though, she's kind of entitled. Sort of bossy, too." She thought of how Hazel gave her kisses that one day and smiled. "But she can be sweet when she wants to be."

"Seems like you spend a lot of time with her."

"She's Wes's favorite. He watches her, like, almost every day."

Max nodded thoughtfully. "You like working for him?"

"Yeah, it's all right."

"It's just, he seems kind of . . . weird. Grumpy," Max persisted.

"I think he's just lonely. All he has are the dogs."

"Wasn't he married before? Loral—I mean, I heard he was married, and his wife left him."

Jessie pictured Wes at dinner with his ex-wife, the way they sat together in the corner, so focused on each other they hadn't noticed her staring at them.

"What?" Max asked.

"What do you mean, what?" Jessie asked, as innocently as she could.

"You're making a weird face."

"Maybe that's just my face."

Max laughed. "Fine then. Don't tell me. I don't care."

"Yes, you do, or you wouldn't have asked."

"Eh, I'm over it now."

Jessie scowled. "I saw him out at dinner with his ex-wife," she burst out, and suddenly she was telling Max all about it, as if the story had been cooking inside her for days, and now that she'd started talking, there was no way to put a lid back on it. "I recognized her from the picture he has on his refrigerator," she finished.

Max tilted his head to the side. "He has a picture of his ex-wife on his refrigerator," he said slowly. "That's kind of strange, isn't it?"

"I think it's sad, not strange." Jessie thought of the pictures her dad kept of her mom. Sometimes he turned them over, too, when he couldn't bear to look at her, but he never got rid of them. "I don't think he's ready to let go of her yet," she decided, and for a second, she wasn't sure if she was thinking of her dad or Wes. She gave herself a little shake. "Anyhow, I'm pretty sure he actually misses his old dog the most. That's got to be why he won't get another dog of his own." She pictured Wes sitting in his chair, his eyes closed and hand resting on Hazel's furry little head. *Everyone leaves you eventually.* Would another dog of his own help him move on?

Or would it just remind him of what he was missing?

Jessie scuffed her feet along the sidewalk. For the first time, she wondered if getting a dog would make her miss her mom more, too. She'd always pictured them walking her dog together. That would never happen now. It would just be her. All the responsibility would be on her. When she went back home, she wouldn't have Wes to help, and her dad would be too busy.

"Well, if Wes gets too strange for you," Max said, "my mom could take you on, if you want—"

"No, I'm good. Thanks." Up ahead, Jessie could see Ann's house, all lit up and waiting. She had a sudden urge to sprint for it.

"You know . . ." Max began slowly, deliberately, every word dropping like pebbles into a pond, "Wes isn't doing too well. I mean, I don't know what he's told you, but a lot of his clients aren't that happy with him. They've been hiring my mom instead."

And just like that, the last of Jessie's relaxed happiness vanished. "You mean she's been stealing them," she said coldly.

"What? No. She's not *stealing* them. She's just . . . letting them know what they're missing, being with someone like Wes, when they could be with her."

"You mean someone who's more focused on taking cute little pictures than the walks themselves?"

Max's face darkened. "And what's wrong with pictures? They make people happy, don't they?"

Jessie stopped walking and put her hands on her hips. "She should care more about the *dogs'* happiness. But she doesn't even seem to like them much."

"She does *so* like dogs."

"No, she owned a dog and made it sound like it was a huge hassle."

"Dogs *are* a hassle!"

"Wes doesn't think so. He loves dogs; they're his whole life! And she's trying to ruin that."

"She needs the business! She needs to make a living here, too, you know." Now Max's hands were on his hips, too. "And she knows Wes is up to something. He's messing with her stuff. She *knows* it."

Jessie felt the guilt crawling across her face, but she passed it off as anger. "Maybe she should just leave him alone, then. Just go off and start a new business."

"She can't do that. She's put too much time and money into this one."

"That's her problem."

"It's *not* a problem, because she's doing just fine. And even if she wasn't, what other kind of business could she start?"

"She can . . . I don't know, walk cats or something."

"Cats?" Max raised his eyebrows. "That's your idea of a successful business? Cat walking?"

"She wouldn't have any competition." She imagined Monique walking a pack of cats, all meowing and trying to climb trees and dart under bushes. It was hard to stay angry, picturing that.

Max seemed to be struggling, too. His lips curved up in a small, amused smile. "That's very true. Not a lot of competition in the cat-walking department." He began walking again, and Jessie fell into step next to him. "Let's not fight about this. I promised my mom I would ask you if you wanted to work with her, and I've done that. Clearly you don't." He shrugged.

"OK then," Jessie said.

"OK," Max agreed. They got to Ann's doorstep and he stopped and looked at her. "I had a nice time, mostly."

"I did, too. Mostly."

"Friends?" He put out his hand.

Jessie stared at it. What was up with this boy and handshakes? And why did she feel strangely . . . disappointed? What had she been expecting? "Sure," she said finally. "But I'm not shaking your hand. I don't know where it's been."

He grinned. "You don't *want* to know."

Jessie wrinkled her nose. "You're gross."

"Aww, come on, I can't be that bad. You were willing to get ice cream with me."

"My choices were finish washing dishes or eat ice cream. I would have gone with a plague-infested rat."

"Well. It's good to know you have *some* standards."

Jessie smiled. Silence built up around them. She was torn between wanting to go inside, and wanting to stand here, and wanting . . . she wasn't even sure what she wanted.

Max cleared his throat. "Well. I'd better walk home. Getting late."

"Getting late," she agreed.

Max moved closer, and Jessie's breath caught in her throat.

"Soccer tomorrow?" he asked. "Meet me at the park at ten? I . . . I've missed playing you, Jessie."

Jessie. The way he said her name made her feel all tingly inside. "O-OK. Tomorrow morning," she said. "But you'd better actually be there this time."

"I'll be there. I promise."

And then he was gone, and she could breathe again. She headed into the house, her stomach flip-flopping, turning her ice cream into a milkshake inside her. But she was just excited about soccer in the morning. That was it. Just soccer.

CHAPTER 26

I don't know, Jessie, sounds like it was a date." Ann fiddled with her bangs, straightening them and then curling the ends under.

"Can't be. He's still dating Loralee." Jessie kicked her feet back and forth. For once, she was happy to sit on her cot in Ann's room as the morning drifted lazily by. She had plenty of time to get to the park and nowhere to be before then. "Has . . . has Loralee mentioned if they've been having problems?"

"No. But we haven't really talked much lately." Ann turned away from her dresser mirror.

Jessie immediately felt bad. "I'm sorry, I wasn't—"

"It's OK. It's just . . . I miss hanging out with her."

"Well, you'll get to hang out today. Aren't you so lucky," Jessie added drily.

Ann flashed her a smile, which Jessie returned. While Jessie couldn't think of anything worse than spending a day with Loralee, she knew her cousin was looking forward to it. She could tell, because Ann had changed her shirt about seven times until she was sure she had the right outfit, and she'd spent forever on her makeup. What a waste of time.

"Well, I'd better run." Ann hesitated. "You still sure about that outfit? I mean, this *could* be a second date . . ."

Jessie threw a pillow at her. "It's not a date. It's just soccer."

"I don't know, he might score a goal and then try to kiss you."

Jessie threw her other pillow.

Ann caught it, laughing. "Fine, fine. Good luck anyways." She left, her laughter echoing down the hall.

Jessie shook her head. Ann was being completely ridiculous. Max had said "friends." She wasn't even going to waste another second thinking about kisses. And anyhow, he was with Loralee. But then, he had seemed pretty annoyed about her possessiveness . . . Maybe they would break up soon?

Immediately, guilt slammed into Jessie, and she tried to push those thoughts away. Even if it was Loralee, that wasn't fair.

But thirty minutes later, she couldn't get the thought out of her head. What if he *did* break up with Loralee and then tried to kiss her? Would she let him? Did she want him to? She thought of his fox smile, those dimples, the way his brown eyes crinkled at the edges . . . She wasn't sure what she wanted, but her stomach felt all queasy and her skin was hot. She walked slowly to the park, kicking her soccer ball along, and for once, she didn't notice the dogs she passed.

As she kicked the ball around and did a few sprints and

stretches to warm up, she kept getting distracted. Every person that came near was Max . . . until they turned out not to be. Every footstep had her whipping around. Every voice had her jumping.

"Calm, confident energy," Jessie told herself firmly as she stretched her hamstrings. She was being silly. If she wasn't careful, she'd turn into Ann-Marie. Or even worse: She'd become like Loralee. Jessie shuddered. Never. She'd never be like her.

And where was Max, anyhow? She knew it was way after ten. As the minutes ticked by and she got tired of warming up, she stopped wondering if he might try to kiss her and started wondering if he would even bother to show up.

Footsteps crunched through the grass toward her. Her heart sped up, and she turned. "Finally—"

But it still wasn't Max. It was Ann. Ann, looking small. Looking crumpled.

"I just," Ann stopped, took a breath. "I didn't want you waiting here too long. So, I thought I should find you. Max isn't coming." She sniffed. "I'm sorry, Jessie. I guess he's . . . he's with Loralee."

Jessie felt frozen. He had promised to meet her. He had said "friends." And yet, once again, he had ditched her for Loralee. Jessie realized "frozen" was not the right word at all. No, she was burning, burning with anger.

"He's not worth it, Jessie," Ann said. "Anyone who stands you up like that is not worth your time."

Jessie picked up her soccer ball and squeezed it, imagining it was Max's head. His stupid head with his stupid fox smile. "Ouch," she whispered. Soccer balls were not very squeezable.

"Let's go home, OK? We can . . . we can watch a movie, if you want? Anything but *Die Hard*."

Jessie nodded, silently following her cousin home. She didn't really feel like watching a movie, but as she walked she realized: She wasn't the only one who'd been stood up. Again. She watched Ann out of the corner of her eye, and her anger drained away, replaced by . . . Jessie wasn't sure, exactly. But when they got home, she let Ann choose the movie, and even though it was a terrible romantic comedy, she didn't complain.

CHAPTER 27

Sunday came and went. With no dogs to walk and no soccer to play, Jessie didn't see much point in getting out of bed.

"You can't just mope all day." Ann yanked the covers off Jessie. "No moping. Also your dad's on the phone."

That got Jessie up. Her dad couldn't talk long but wanted to let her know that everything was going great. "Swimmingly, really," he assured her. "How are things in the dog-walking business?"

She thought of Wes, and how they'd sabotaged Monique, and paused. "G-good."

"Hmm. Not having second thoughts about that dog, are you?"

"Of course not," Jessie said quickly. This was what she wanted. Wasn't it?

"Great. Because I've already picked one out for you."

Jessie dropped the phone.

"Hello? Hello? Jess?"

She scrambled to pick it up. "You got me a dog?" she whispered. "Really?" Her whisper turned into a squeak.

"Well, I haven't picked her up yet. I'm planning on getting her on my way out to get you in a couple weeks. So if you don't want her . . ."

"I do! I want her!" Jessie danced in place, so happy she thought she might explode with it. Then reality trickled in. "What kind of dog?"

Her dad laughed. "It's a breed you told me about."

"I've told you about a lot of different kinds of dogs."

"I know. I'm letting it be a surprise." Jessie could hear the smile in his voice. "Now, she's young, but she's not exactly a puppy, OK? I thought about it, but there are so many dogs who need homes. This particular one was adopted out once before, but it didn't work out, so she was taken in by a rescue."

"Didn't work out?" Jessie's heart clenched. Poor little pup.

"Apparently her original owners didn't have enough time for her." He sighed, his voice getting super serious. "So, I want you to be sure you want her, OK? That you'll make the time for her. Because I will be busy working, and I promised she'd be in the best home."

The best home. Would that be with Jessie? She thought suddenly of Monique. *I wanted a dog when I was younger, too. It was a lot more work than I thought.* But Jessie already knew dogs were a lot of work, and she was ready for it. She could take a dog out for a walk before school and then right after. She could skip soccer games, and soccer camp, and hanging out with her friends. Dogs were better than people anyhow. And if she wanted to provide the best home, she'd have to be as devoted to dogs as Wes was. She could do that, couldn't she?

"Well, kiddo, I gotta run. Love you."

"Love you back," Jessie said.

Click. Jessie stared at the phone for a long time and then hung up in a daze.

"You OK?" Ann asked.

"Dad got me a dog. He actually did it."

"Really? That's great. I'm really happy for you, Jessie." Ann smiled, and it was so like the old Ann that Jessie's heart ached.

"You . . . wanna watch a movie?" Jessie asked, and Ann's smile widened.

"I thought you'd never ask."

Jessie spent the rest of the day hanging out with Ann, and surprisingly it wasn't terrible. They walked to the candy store, just like they used to; watched a bunch of movies, most of them with explosions and chase scenes but a couple with kissing, too, to keep Ann happy; and then ended the day with a bike ride followed by a few video games. Jessie lost every single one. She wasn't good at anything that involved sitting around. But it was still fun, and she didn't think of Max once the whole day. OK, maybe once. Or twice. But definitely no more than a dozen times. And when Monday morning rolled around, she'd completely banished him from her thoughts forever.

She got to Wes's house right on time, but he wasn't out on his porch. That wasn't terribly unusual. Bursting with her news about her own dog, Jessie knocked rapidly and waited, shifting her weight onto the balls of her feet and lifting her heels up and down. She'd spent too much time sitting this weekend and had a ton of energy to burn.

"Hello! Wes?" She knocked again, louder.

Nothing.

Frowning, Jessie pounded on the door one more time and put her ear to it. Still nothing. Maybe he'd headed out early?

"You're Wes's little helper, aren't you?" a man asked.

Jessie turned. The man behind her was very tall, with hunched shoulders, his gray hair streaked with white. It took her a minute, but then she remembered. "Angel."

"That's right, Angel's my dog, and the reason I'm here." The man glanced around, as if ensuring his wife wasn't hiding in the bushes, and then whispered, "You were absolutely right. We made a mistake switching. Do you think Wes will take us back? I left him a message yesterday but haven't heard back."

"I . . . I'm sure he will," Jessie said, trying to keep her voice level. Calm. Professional.

"Can he start today? Angel misses him."

"Sure, I'll tell him for you. He'll be happy to have him back."

The man relaxed. "That's great. Thank you."

When he was gone, Jessie tried knocking again. Wes's car was there in the driveway. He *had* to be around. She would just knock until he came out, or his door splintered.

KNOCK-KNOCK-KNOCK-KNOCK-KNOCK.

The door flew open. Wes's hair was a tangle around his head, his shirt was wrinkled, and he wore a pair of faded old sweatpants. "Go. Away."

He slammed the door so hard it opened again, and Jessie caught the edge. "It's dog walking tim—"

"I DON'T CARE WHAT TIME IT IS," he roared. "I'm done, you hear me? I'm done."

"But the dogs—"

"Can walk themselves, for all I care." He grabbed a shoe off the rack by his door and chucked it over her head. Jessie let go of the door, and he slammed it shut and locked it.

She stared at it. This . . . was not normal. Even for Wes. He was often openly hostile, but it was never about the dogs. She raised her hand to knock, then hesitated and looked back at the shoe lying out in the middle of the yard. It had missed her by inches. Maybe . . . maybe it would be better to let Wes cool down a little. Give him some space.

She pictured Angel, waiting for his walk.

Jessie sighed and adjusted her hip pack. She could take care of Angel herself and then come back. By then, Wes would be ready. He'd have to be.

But Wes *wasn't* ready when she got back. Not even close. Jessie pounded on the door so long her hand ached and a neighbor yelled at her, and Wes never showed. What was going on with him? And what should she do?

She thought of all the Rules. This seemed like a case for Rule Number Four: Always be ready. She couldn't let the dogs down. There was only one thing to do: She'd have to walk them herself.

But . . . she didn't have a car.

Jessie hesitated, then looked down at her feet. Always be ready.

She always was.

CHAPTER 28

Jessie slowly trudged home, her whole body aching. She had never been so tired in her entire life, but she'd done it. She'd walked every single dog on Wes's list, running to each house in between. Dogs who lived close enough were combined, but since she was on foot, most had to be walked individually. It made for a very long, very exhausting day. Her stomach was beyond empty, and a quick glance at her wristwatch told her it was already after five.

She patted her trusty hip pack as she walked. It had served her well, but it would be nice to take it off.

Wes's house loomed just up ahead, and Jessie hesitated. Should she check on him? Or just leave him alone?

She chewed her lip and decided she'd at least swing by. Maybe he'd be feeling better and could tell her how amazing she was for doing all the dogs on her own. She shook her head. This was Wes; he'd probably call her an irritating child and send her out the door. Still, secretly he'd be proud, she knew.

But when she got to his house, she found she wasn't the only one trying to visit.

Hazel's mom stood on the doorstep in jeans and a wrinkled shirt, her reddish-blond hair tumbling around her shoulders in a frizzy mess of curls. It was strange; she normally looked so elegant.

"Can I help you?" Jessie asked.

The woman spun and put a hand to her mouth, her eyes wide and startled. "You're . . . you're the girl who's working with Wes, right?" she asked, lowering her hand.

Jessie nodded. "And you're Hazel's mom."

"Right. Diana." She smiled, but it was over quickly, a reflex, not an emotion. "I've been trying to reach Wes all day, to explain, but he's not answering. Do you know if he's home?"

Suspicion pooled in the pit of Jessie's stomach and congealed there like a bite of her aunt's meatloaf. "Explain?" she asked slowly.

"Well, I, um . . . maybe I should just come back later?" Diana glanced back at the closed door, then at Jessie.

Jessie shifted just enough to block the porch stairs. "You didn't hire another dog walker for Hazel, did you?"

Diana's eyes widened. "Um, I thought . . ." She stopped, pulled herself up straighter. "I thought it would be for the best."

Oh no. Oh no. Jessie clutched at the banister for support. This . . . this would destroy Wes.

"Monique talked to me this weekend," Diana continued.

"H-how do you know Monique?" Jessie's ears filled with the pounding of her pulse until it felt like she was underwater. Was this really happening?

"Everyone knows Monique. And apparently Monique knows everyone," she added, sniffing. "Including Sarah. Who Monique saw with Wes last week. On a date." She sniffed again.

"A . . . a date?" Jessie's voice was a whisper, a husk, a shell.

Diana seemed to crumble around the edges until she was as small and insubstantial as Jessie's voice. "I thought he was moving on, but how is getting dinner with your ex moving on? And the picture . . ." She took a deep, shuddering breath. "Monique was right about that, too. He still has a picture of Sarah on his fridge. How can we . . . I mean." She rubbed her eyes. "It would be better if he didn't watch Hazel anymore, if we cut all ties for now. Better for both of us, he'll see it's better . . . I just need a chance to explain . . ." Jessie realized Diana was talking to herself now, which was for the best; all of Jessie's words had turned to ash in her mouth, choking her. All she could think was: her fault, her fault, her fault.

He has a picture of his ex-wife on his refrigerator.

She had told Max that, *she* had told him about the maybe-date. She'd given him all the information his mom needed to bring down Wes.

Hazel is Wes's favorite. He watches her, like, almost every day.

Her fault. Her fault. *Her fault.*

CHAPTER 29

Jessie ran. She wasn't sure where she was running, or why, she just knew her feet needed to move, her body needed to move, *she* needed to move. Her earlier exhaustion had dropped away, her hunger was forgotten. She was just wind and sweat and pumping arms.

But no matter how hard she ran, how fast, she couldn't feel empty. Her head was so full of hurt it spilled down into her heart. Her fault.

She had betrayed Wes.

Jessie's feet slowed. She blinked blurry eyes and realized she'd ended up at the park. Of course, she had. Where else would her feet have taken her?

Jessie sat on the closest bench and put her head in her hands. She'd have to go home soon, or she'd get in trouble, and she couldn't afford that. If Wes wasn't up for dog walking tomorrow, she'd have to take over again. It was her fault he'd lost Hazel; she couldn't let him lose anyone else.

Her fault.

How did everything get so tangled? Obviously Diana

liked Wes, and Jessie was pretty sure Wes liked her back. And Jessie had gone and messed all that up. Worse, without Hazel, Wes didn't have a dog anymore. Again. She couldn't stop thinking of him sitting in his chair, Hazel on his lap, both of them with their eyes half-closed. *Everyone leaves you eventually.*

Jessie thought she might throw up.

"Do you, like, live in the park now?"

Jessie slowly lifted her head, her body filling with that same nameless dread it always did when she heard Loralee's voice.

The dread intensified into something harder and fiercer when she saw . . .

"Max." She said his name like a swear word, and he flinched and looked away, his fingers entwined with Loralee's. Jessie stood up, her body stiff and cold despite the late afternoon heat. "You . . . you . . ." She couldn't even find the words.

Loralee pursed her glossy lips and looked back and forth between the two of them, then laughed. "Oh, Jessie," she purred. "Jessie, Jessie, Jessie. You didn't think Max *really* wanted to hang out with you, did you? He was just trying to get information."

"Hey, that's not really . . ." Max began. Loralee's fingers tightened around his, and he stopped and looked down at his feet.

Jessie's eyes filled with tears, and she ran the back of her hand across her face.

"See, I told you. She's such a child," Loralee stage-whispered.

"You don't have to be nasty about it," Max said, but he didn't let go of her hand. "Look, Jess, it wasn't . . . I mean, my mom asked me to do it. She's my mom. I had to. But I . . . I didn't mean . . ."

Jessie didn't, *couldn't*, say anything.

He shuffled his feet. "I didn't think I told her anything that important."

"Maybe we should just go," Loralee said.

Max ignored her. "Look, Jessie, I'm sorry."

That apology knocked something loose inside Jessie. Her tears dried up and she looked him full in the face. "I hate you." The words tumbled from her mouth like an avalanche. She was shaking. She'd never said those words to anyone. Not ever. Not even Loralee.

Max's eyes widened, his cheeks reddening like she'd just slapped him.

She turned and walked away. Her ears were ringing, and she felt impossibly light, like all her insides had been scooped out and replaced by nothingness.

Along the way her inner mantra changed.

Her fault. Her fault. *His* fault.

CHAPTER 30

Tuesday morning, Jessie dragged herself out of bed. This time she borrowed Ann's spare bike, throwing her hip pack and spare leashes on the basket in front before riding over to Wes's house. She tried rehearsing what she would say, but once she reached his doorstep, all her pretty words dried in her mouth. She made herself knock anyway. And knock again. And keep knocking.

"Go away," Wes said from behind his door.

"I need to talk to you." Jessie kicked his door. Her hand was starting to hurt.

A few minutes later, she stopped. Clearly Wes was never going to open his door again. She could picture it nailed shut, wood boards crisscrossed in front of it, chains rattling around the doorknob.

She sighed and sat on his porch, the early morning cloudy and cold as it pressed around her. Her gaze dropped to the ceramic coaster Wes always left out here. It looked dusty, the blue-gray pattern so faded that she wasn't sure what it was supposed to resemble. All she was sure of was that Wes had to start walking dogs again, because the end of summer wasn't that far away. Soon Jessie would be leaving behind all her old friends, Angel and Sweetpea and all the others. She needed to make sure they were in good hands. She needed to make sure they were with Wes.

She thought back through all the Rules of the Ruff, but none of them really covered a situation like this. How could you make someone listen to you if they didn't want to?

Creak.

Jessie leapt to her feet.

Wes stood in his doorway, his hair a tangle around his head, his clothes wrinkled and smelling none too clean. "What part of 'go away' did you not understand? The 'go'? Or the 'away'?"

Jessie cringed. Wes being rude was nothing new, but the fury radiating off him made her feel like she was standing next to an angry sun. "I don't understand the why," she managed, her throat tight.

Wes glared at her, and she noticed how puffy his eyes looked. Almost like he'd been crying. Did . . . did adults cry?

A flash of memory. Her father clutching her mother's favorite shirt, his face scrunched, body curled around it like it was a living thing he had to protect . . .

Jessie dropped that memory as fast as she could.

"'The why'?" Wes demanded.

"W-why are you hiding out in there? Your dogs need you."

He snorted. "They've moved on to bigger and better things."

"Do you know what Monique said about the dogs?" Jessie demanded.

"I'm sure I don't care."

"She said they were 'just dogs.' Does that sound like bigger or better to you? She doesn't love them, not like you do. And Hazel . . ." Wes flinched as if she'd struck him, and she hurried on. "Hazel loves you, I know she does. I know she misses you." Jessie took a deep breath. "Please, Wes. At least try to get her back. So many of the others have come back to you. Don't give up. Would . . . would a dog give up?"

He stared at her, his eyes narrowing. "Get her back?" he asked softly.

"She misses you," Jessie repeated.

It looked like he was really considering it, like Jessie had actually reached him, but then he just stepped back inside and shut the door in her face.

Jessie yelped, almost tumbling backward off the porch steps. "Fine!" she shouted. "See if I care!" She wiped at her face, because she was not crying. She was not crying. She was . . .

She was definitely crying. But she couldn't decide if it was because she was sad or angry. She just knew it wasn't fair, none of this was fair, and she didn't know how to fix it, and it was all her fault. Sniffing, she wiped her face on her shirt and picked up Ann's bike.

Maybe she really should just give up, go home, go back to bed. She thought of the third Rule of the Ruff: Know when to leave it. Maybe . . . maybe this was one of those times?

Jessie hesitated. And then she remembered something else, something Wes had said a while back. *Some dogs will sit in the same spots, staring at their front doors all day long, just waiting for their owners to show up.* She shook her head. She couldn't do that to them, couldn't leave them waiting like that. She would continue to walk these dogs until Wes took over, or until her dad came and picked her up.

CHAPTER 31

That night, Jessie ate everything her aunt put in front of her, didn't say anything all through the meal, and went right to bed afterward. Ann tried asking her if she was all right, but Jessie didn't have language for how she was feeling, like she was the last dregs of a soap bottle and someone kept adding water to keep her going.

She fell asleep with that image in her mind and slept soundly and dreamlessly until the beeping of the alarm woke her the next morning. Before she could move, Ann turned it off.

"Thanks," Jessie mumbled, struggling to get out of bed. Everything hurt. Her arms were so tired from holding all those leashes, she thought they might fall right off her shoulders. And her legs . . . she didn't even want to think about her legs. Biking had not been kind to her. And her butt. Oh, her butt. She groaned. And she had Angel to walk first thing this morning.

Jessie glanced outside Ann's bedroom window. The sky was already a deep gray, heavy with the threat of rain. It looked like her heart.

"What is going on with you?" Ann asked.

"Nothing."

"Really? Because a whole lot of 'nothing' seems to have hit you like a bus." Ann turned on the light, and Jessie squinted against it. "Last night, you ate my mom's cooking and didn't complain at all. And I *know* she put extra onions in it. I watched her do it."

Jessie felt ill. "Why? Why would she do that?"

Ann shrugged. "The point is, you didn't notice. You just ate it. And then you slept like you were dead. So. What are you up to? Does this have something to do with the dogs? With Max?"

"Don't you say his name!" Jessie snapped, exhaustion evaporating in a burst of fury. "I don't ever want to hear his name again."

Ann blinked. "Whoa. OK, clearly *something* happened." She leaned forward. "Tell me about it."

"I don't want to talk about it." Jessie looked away, chewing her lip.

"Fine. I didn't want to hear about it anyhow."

"Yeah, you did."

"No, it's probably boring stuff." Ann looked down at her nails, clearly already bored.

"It's not boring!" Jessie scowled at her cousin and then found herself spilling the whole story, from Max asking her questions about Wes's ex-wife to Diana taking Hazel away. "I can't let Wes lose his business, too. I have to keep walking dogs for him until he gets over it, or he'll have nothing left," she finished.

Ann smiled.

"What's funny?" Jessie demanded. "This is very serious, very not-boring stuff."

"You're funny. That reverse psychology stuff always works on you."

"It does not—" Jessie stopped, her heart sinking. "OK, maybe sometimes it works," she admitted.

"If by 'sometimes' you mean 'always,' then yes." Ann's smile widened. "But I'm glad. And I'm glad you told me. It's definitely not boring, and Ma—er, he who must not be named, is a total jerk."

Even Jessie had to smile at that reference.

"So I've decided," Ann said, "that I'll help you."

"Y-you'll . . . what?"

"I'll help you walk the dogs."

"I don't need any help."

"Jessie, you're going to kill yourself. And I . . ." She fiddled with her hair, not looking up. "I don't really have anything else to do."

Jessie remembered how she'd felt at the start of summer, like she was staring at an impossibly large, impossibly boring blank page. *Yeah, and whose fault was that?* Ann had chosen to hang out with Loralee instead of with her.

She opened her mouth to say that, then stopped. Wes's words echoed through her head: *Everyone leaves you eventually*, and she pictured him sitting there, alone. No Hazel, no Diana, nothing but his LEGO sets to keep him company, his door shut and locked against the rest of the world.

Maybe sometimes people could come back to you, too. If you let them.

"All right, you can help," Jessie decided.

"Really?" Ann's whole face lit up. She must have been really bored.

"Yes. But only on one condition." Jessie couldn't stop the smile that spread across her face as she said, "You'll have to master the Rules of the Ruff."

"The what of the what?"

"You'll have to learn to think like a dog, to act like a dog, to be a dog."

Ann shook her head. "You are such a weirdo. But fine. I'm in."

"Let's get started." Jessie thought of their first walk of the day and chuckled. "I have just the dog for you . . ."

"Calm, confident energy, Ann," Jessie instructed.

"I *am* calm." Ann's voice was strained, her arms shaking as she held on to the leash. "Don't I look calm?"

"Who's walking who?" a passerby asked.

Ann's mouth fell open and she turned to Jessie. "Why would someone even *ask* that?"

Jessie shrugged. "Get used to it. It gets worse."

"Hey there, little lady. Need a sled?" someone else called as they jogged past.

Ann's nostrils flared. "I'll give you a sled," she muttered.

"Easy there, *little lady*." Jessie giggled.

"Watch it—oof!" Angel lunged forward, dragging Ann until she managed to get her feet under her and pull back on the leash.

"Calm, confident energy," Jessie repeated, grinning. This *was* a lot of fun. No wonder Wes had taken her on.

Wes.

Her grin melted away faster than ice cream on a hot summer day, and she picked up her pace. They still had a lot of dogs to cover.

"Are we almost done?" Ann yelled over the sound of the wind a few hours later. "I'm c-cold!"

"One more walk." One more walk, and they would be successfully done for the day. Jessie felt really proud of that and also proud of how well Ann had just walked Luke and Leia, their cottony fur soaking up the rain and leaving them sad and bedraggled. She was even more proud of how Ann had carefully toweled them off at the house until they were close to their old fluffy selves. Ann might claim she didn't love dogs because they were "too slobbery," "too hyper," or "too covered in all that dog fur," but Jessie could tell they were winning her cousin over.

It wasn't like it used to be, her and Ann. They weren't pretending to be ninjas or pirates or ninja pirates. In fact, any mention of make-believe made Ann uncomfortable, but Jessie realized they were still able to talk and laugh and walk dogs and have a good time together. It would never be quite like it was, but maybe that was OK, too.

"OK, who do we have?" Ann asked.

"Pickles, Zelda, and I thought we'd pick up Presto along the way and just walk him extra."

Ann nodded. "Sounds doable."

The rain picked up, each droplet larger and colder than the one before. Jessie and Ann looked at each other. "Run over?" Jessie suggested.

"Run over," Ann agreed. And then they were sprinting and laughing as they charged head first into the rain. Even the sight of Monique up ahead couldn't ruin Jessie's good mood.

"What's she doing?" Ann asked, and Jessie realized: Monique didn't have a dog with her. Instead, she was running with an empty leash in one hand, running in a weird, zigzagging pattern, her eyes flicking all over the place.

"I . . . have no idea. Let's just get this last walk done."

"A-agreed." Ann shivered, and they picked up the pace. But all through that last walk, Jessie kept picturing Monique, the way she'd been so frantically searching, an empty leash in her hand.

CHAPTER 32

The next morning dawned bright and beautiful, with barely a hint of the rain from the day before. Jessie woke up early, no alarm needed. Across the room, Ann slept soundly, her hand flung over her face. After a few seconds of deliberating, Jessie left her sleeping. Sure, she'd offered to help yesterday, but Jessie doubted her cousin would want to spend another full day with her and the dogs.

Jessie decided not to bother with Wes this morning; she didn't feel like wasting her time. Instead, she headed straight for Angel's house.

"Hey! You jerk!"

Jessie turned, surprised to see Ann running toward her in an overlarge jacket and sweatpants, her long blond hair trailing unbrushed behind her. "Ann?"

"You didn't wake me up!" Ann caught up, then bent over, panting for breath. "I heard the front door close and had to hurry after you." She straightened. "Why didn't you wake me?"

"I didn't think you'd want to walk dogs again."

Ann crossed her arms. "Why wouldn't I want to? I mean, I've practically mastered these dog rules—"

"Rules of the Ruff, and no you haven't."

"Well, I'm getting close. I figure another day or two and I'll have them down."

"It might take longer than that," Jessie warned.

Ann shrugged. "We'll see. I'm a fast learner."

"Loralee might break up with . . . might be free again before you become an expert."

"Actually, they already broke up," Ann said carefully.

"What? They *did?*" Jessie coughed. "I mean, not that I care." Max could go ahead and marry Loralee, and it wouldn't bother her one little bit.

"Yeah, Loralee actually wanted to hang out today, but I told her I was busy."

"Really?"

"Really," Ann said.

Jessie hadn't realized how knotted up her stomach was, but it loosened now. She pictured it as a nest of snakes, all trapped in a basket, and someone had lifted the lid. Just an inch. Just enough for a snake or two to escape.

"You've got that weird look on your face," Ann said. "Like you're thinking weird thoughts."

"This is just how my face always looks." Jessie pushed all images of snakes and baskets from her head. Even though they weren't weird thoughts; lots of people probably pictured snakes in their stomachs. Probably.

As they rounded the corner, she saw something that made her forget about snakes entirely.

Wes was standing outside Angel's house. Wes, his hair brushed, his clothing clean, wearing his standard hip pack. Looking like himself, like he hadn't spent the past few days hiding out in his house.

"Hey kid. I thought I might run into you here." He smiled. Actually smiled.

Jessie realized her mouth was hanging open, and she shut it. "H-hey. I, uh, brought on an assistant."

Wes's smile dropped. "Another assistant." He narrowed his eyes at Ann, who shrank behind Jessie. "Hmm. Doesn't look very helpful."

"She's been a lot more helpful than you this week."

Wes laughed once, loud and sharp like a dog's bark. "Fine. I guess you're off poop-scooping duty today, then."

"What does that mean?" Ann whispered.

Jessie hesitated. "It means . . . you're probably going to regret joining me today."

"There's another one." Jessie pointed to a pile, grinning.

Ann rolled her eyes, but she cleaned it up. "You are going to pay for this," she muttered.

"Probably." Jessie couldn't stop smiling, though. Wes was back to his old unpleasant self, Ann was stuck cleaning up after the dogs, and things were all right with the world. Plus, they were almost done already, and it was barely noon. It was amazing how much faster the walks went when you had three people and a car.

"Garbage over there." Jessie pointed, and Ann, still muttering, headed toward it.

"Hey, Jessie?" Ann called. "Did you see this?"

"What's your minion on about?" Wes asked.

Jessie shrugged but maneuvered her pair of cattle dogs over toward Ann, who was pointing at a sign taped to the tree beside her.

"Have you seen me?" Jessie read the block letters, then looked at the photograph. All the air vanished from her lungs.

Hazel's distinctive little wolfy face stared back, those big brown eyes full of entitlement, that little snout lifted slightly in the air. "Oh. Oh no." Jessie closed her eyes, remembering Monique running yesterday, an empty leash in her hand. "Wes." She tried to shout his name, but it just came out in a whisper.

"What is it, kiddo?" He read the sign, and his face went blank. It was like staring at a robot, no expression at all.

"We need to look for her," Jessie said. "We need to—hey!"

Wes had ripped the page off the tree and crumpled it. He shook himself, as if coming to his senses. "We'll keep an eye out as we walk. I'm sure she'll turn up." He stuffed the crumpled page deep into his pocket and then marched his pack up ahead.

He didn't say anything else about it, not a single word. Nothing as they finished the walk or as they dropped off the dogs. Maybe his worry went beyond words.

"All right, kiddo, enjoy your weekend," he said as he parked his car.

"It's only Thursday," Jessie pointed out.

"I'll cover tomorrow myself. You've earned a day off.

Come back normal time Monday." He glanced at Ann. "You can tag along again if you must."

"Don't count on it," Ann muttered.

"Wes . . ." Jessie hesitated. "About Hazel—"

"She'll turn up," he said abruptly. "Very irresponsible of Monique, though. Bet Diana is really sorry she switched dog walkers now."

"I bet Diana is really sorry her dog is missing," Jessie said softly.

Wes's face drooped. "Yeah, she probably is." He slammed his car door shut and went inside his house without another word.

Jessie and Ann exchanged looks and started back to the house. "Is it just me, or was he being super weird?" Ann asked.

"He's always super weird."

"I got that. But, I thought Hazel was his favorite dog ever."

"She was. Is."

"You'd think he'd be more worried about her, then."

Jessie wasn't sure what to say to that, either, but she noticed several more missing dog posters along the way back to Ann's house. Each one felt like a punch to the stomach. How could Monique have lost a dog? She could picture little Hazel out in the rain, lost, alone, howling her little wolf howl . . .

"Are you crying?" Ann asked.

"No," Jessie sniffled, wiping her face. "I'm just . . . Hazel . . . she's so little."

"Oh, Jessie, I'm sure she'll turn up." Ann wrapped an

arm around Jessie's shoulders and hugged her. "If Wes was so calm about it, it must mean he's sure, too. And he knows dogs better than anyone, right?"

Jessie nodded, but it was hard to make her eyes stop leaking. Her vision was so blurry, she almost didn't notice Max waiting outside Ann's house when they arrived.

"What's wrong?" he asked.

"What are you doing here?" Ann demanded. "Came to spy again?"

Max turned red. "No, of course not. I just wanted to talk to Jessie."

"Well she doesn't want to talk to you, so just run along."

"It's OK, Ann." Jessie sniffed. "I'll talk to him."

"Are you sure?" Ann shot Max a scowl that would have made Wes proud, but at Jessie's nod, she shrugged and headed inside. "Holler if you need me." She closed the door behind her, leaving Jessie to face Max alone.

"I'm sorry to bother you." Max dug his sneaker into the dirt, not looking at her. "I know you hate me now, and I know I deserve it."

"Well, at least you know something." Jessie wiped her face on her sleeve. "Why are you here?"

"Two reasons. First, I came here to apologize—"

"Not forgiven."

He winced. "OK, I was expecting that. Can I at least explain—"

"No." Jessie crossed her arms. At least anger had chased away her tears.

"Fine. OK. Then the second reason I'm here . . ." He took a deep breath. "My mom was wondering if you've seen a dog."

"You mean Hazel?" Jessie's anger evaporated, and she shook her head. "I saw the flyer." She hesitated, but she had to know. "How did it happen?"

"We think she must have gotten out through the car window yesterday. Mom left her in there for a minute to grab a coffee." He took off his hat and scrunched it in his hands, looking miserable. "She's been searching for her ever since."

"I'll look for her, too."

"Thanks. Can you also ask Wes? You know, if he's seen her? He won't talk to me or my mom at all."

"I don't think he has . . ." Jessie trailed off, a sudden suspicion settling over her, as thick and uncomfortable as the layer of loose dog fur in Wes's car. "It was raining yesterday, wasn't it?"

"Pouring."

"And . . . your mom still left the car window open?"

"Just an inch or two. She was worried Hazel wouldn't have any fresh air."

The thought solidified, making Jessie's knees weak and her head spin. "And . . . and she got out still?" she whispered. "Through that little window opening?"

"Must have, right? How else would she have gotten out?"

How else. Jessie thought of the spare key, the one she had stolen, and how Wes was hanging onto it. Wes, who hadn't seemed worried enough about Hazel missing.

She nodded numbly. "I'll ask Wes." Her voice sounded far away in her ears, and she felt like she was still asleep. Maybe she was. Maybe this was a dream. She really, really hoped it was a dream.

CHAPTER 33

Jessie felt odd, detached, like a puppet with broken strings, as she made her way back to Wes's house. Taking a deep breath, she knocked hard on his door. She thought she heard a tiny howl, quickly silenced.

"Who is it?" Wes asked through the door.

"It's me. Jessie."

He opened it a crack, just enough to poke his head out. "Haven't I spent enough time with you today?"

"I need to talk to you."

"Talk to me Monday." He tried shutting the door, but Jessie had already wedged her foot inside. He raised his eyebrows. "You're getting fast at that. Impressive."

"Thank you." Jessie grinned, then caught herself. "Hey, don't try to change the subject. I need to talk to you about Hazel."

"There's nothing to talk about. That is Monique's problem, not mine."

"No, it's your problem, because I know you took her."

Silence. Wes scowled. "I don't know what you're talking about."

"If I'm wrong, then let me in."

"I don't want you in my house."

"Because you've got a stolen dog stashed away in there?"

His scowl deepened. "You're just a kid. What would you know about any of this?"

"I know it's wrong to steal someone's dog."

"I did nothing of the sort. I—hey, would you look at that?" He pointed at something behind Jessie.

She turned and looked, almost as a reflex. The minute she did, Wes kicked her foot away from the door and slammed it shut, locking it. "Argh, I can't believe I fell for that!" Jessie leaned her head against the door, humiliated but not defeated. Not yet.

Jessie spent the rest of the afternoon trying to talk to Wes. She pounded on his front door until his neighbor yelled at her to stop. Then she pounded on his back door until that same neighbor threatened to call the police. That seemed like her cue to go home for dinner, but she vowed to come back early the next morning and corner Wes as he was leaving for his dog walks.

All night she dreamed about Hazel, lost and alone and scared, and the next morning she woke up to sunlight spilling through the curtains and the realization that she'd forgotten to set an alarm. She grabbed her clothes and checked the clock. It read 11:43 A.M.

Jessie froze. How had she slept so late? "Argh, there goes all my plans," she muttered. Wes would be finishing his dog walks by now. But maybe if she hurried, she could still catch him . . .

She shoved her notebook and some supplies in a backpack and rushed out the door.

Wes was already home by the time she got there, his car in the driveway, door closed and locked.

"Darn it," Jessie said, heart sinking. Still, she wasn't going to give up. She had all afternoon.

When Wes didn't answer her knocks, she shoved notes through the gap beneath his back door. Wes shredded them and shoved them back to her. So she wrote new notes and taped them to his windows, where he had no choice but to see them. Notes like, "Don't be a dog thief," "You need to return her," and her personal favorite, "I'll keep hounding you until you do the right thing." Wes merely pulled all the blinds firmly down so he wouldn't be able to see her handiwork.

Jessie stood there in his backyard and glared at the shades, but it didn't do her any good.

"What are you doing?" Ann asked.

Jessie almost fell over. "Don't sneak up on me when I'm working!"

"This is working?" Ann jerked her chin at the stack of paper and pens clutched in Jessie's hands.

"It's step two of a complicated plan, OK?" At Ann's questioning look, Jessie explained the Hazel Situation.

Ann studied her, then looked at the pages taped to Wes's blinded-up windows. "You know, you could just tell Hazel's owner."

"I can't do that! Then she'll know he took her dog."

Ann shrugged.

"You don't understand. He'd lose everything. No one

else is going to let a dog thief walk their dogs. He'd lose the whole business."

"Well, maybe he should," Ann said quietly.

Jessie gaped at her. "You don't really mean that."

"Jess, he did steal someone's dog. And before that, he had you help sabotage someone else's business. Honestly, I question his business ethics. Not to mention his maturity."

"Stop talking like that."

"Like what?"

"Like you're some kind of adult."

Ann sighed. "We all have to grow up eventually. Even you. Especially you."

Before Jessie could ask what *that* was supposed to mean, Ann walked off, leaving her alone in Wes's backyard.

Jessie sat down next to the rosebushes, feeling miserable. She didn't know what to do next. No matter what Ann said, she couldn't turn Wes in, not when this whole mess was her fault. She'd convinced Wes to sabotage Monique. And then she'd given Monique the exact information she needed to get revenge on Wes. But she also couldn't keep her mouth shut, because Hazel needed to go home to her mama.

Jessie just needed to get inside Wes's house somehow and get Hazel back, but he was never going to open his door for her. But maybe . . . maybe she could open the door *herself*. She remembered what Wes had told her on her first day working for him: *Most people keep a key hidden somewhere in their yard*. What if Wes had one, too?

She stood up, brushed herself off, and started searching. Twenty minutes later, however, she was beginning to think this was just another dead end. He didn't have a welcome mat, not surprising, and he had only a handful of flowerpots in his backyard, none of them hiding a key. There weren't any turtles or other statues, and she couldn't reach the top of the door to see if he kept a spare key on the frame.

She circled the house, then stood in front of it, hands on her hips, glaring at that tauntingly locked door. She pictured it as an impenetrable fortress, and she could almost see the moat circling around it, the vines wrapping the front door, the dragon standing guard. A dragon with Wes's face, his deep furrow and wispy hair.

"What are you doing?"

Jessie turned, and suddenly her bad day got even worse. "Loralee," she muttered.

"The one and only." Loralee's lips turned up in a smile, and Jessie noticed they weren't as glossy as normal. In fact, Loralee's whole outfit lacked its usual shine and polish. She was wearing a plain black T-shirt, not even fitted, and a pair of old jeans, her eyes tired and faded without their typical coating of eyeliner and mascara.

Good, Jessie thought vehemently, but she found herself asking, "Is everything OK?" She wasn't sure why.

"Please. Everything's fine. It's always fine. You're a mess, though."

"Me? This is how I always look."

Loralee pursed her lips, then shook her head. "Too easy." She straightened her shoulders. "I've been told that I can sometimes be a little bit mean. Occasionally."

Jessie stared at her. That was a joke, right? "Sometimes? Loralee, you're the meanest person I know."

Loralee's whole body drooped. "You're not the first person to tell me that this week," she whispered, and for a second, she looked like she was going to cry. It was the strangest thing Jessie had ever seen, like a dog learning how to meow. Loralee didn't have feelings. She didn't get sad like normal people. She didn't care if she was mean. Was this some kind of trick?

"I've been t-told . . ." Loralee stopped, took a deep breath. "I've been told," she continued in a smoother voice, "that I should be nicer to people. So I'm trying."

"Are you serious?"

Loralee nodded. "But *some people* make it really hard." Her pointed look made it clear that "some people" meant "Jessie."

"Sorry?"

"No, it's not your fault. Well, it is your fault. If you weren't such a strang— such a unique individual . . . but I'm going to be nicer. I really am." She sighed. "Have you seen Max lately, by the way?"

"Not since yesterday. Why?"

"No reason." She inspected her nails as if she couldn't care less, but for once, Jessie could see right through that act. "Just, if you see him again, would you mention that I'm being nicer?"

"Are you?"

"I'm trying!" Loralee snapped. "God, isn't it supposed to be the thought that counts? Why is everyone so judgmental lately?" And then she did burst into tears.

Jessie gaped, not sure what she should do. She thought of her list of ways to get revenge on Loralee, but watching her cry didn't make Jessie feel any better. "H-hey, it's OK."

"How do you know? You don't know anything," Loralee bawled. "You're just a child."

That brought back Jessie's anger. "I'm not the one crying like a baby."

Loralee's eyes widened in surprise, and she hiccuped, her tears slowing. Carefully, she wiped her face on the end of her T-shirt. "Anyway," she managed, her voice hitching, "I really am trying to be nicer. I'm sorry if you were upset before by anything that I said."

Jessie frowned. "Don't you mean you're sorry you said mean things to me?"

"Same thing."

"Not exactly," Jessie said, but looking at Loralee, at her red eyes and blotchy skin and badly fitting clothes, she realized this was the closest thing to an apology she was going to get. She sighed. "I don't know why Max would tell you to be nicer, though. He sure isn't."

"Are you talking about the whole standing you up thing?" Loralee asked softly. "Because . . . that was my fault." She sniffed. "I didn't like him spending so much time with you. I told him he had to choose."

"Why?"

She rubbed her nose and looked away. "He liked you," she said. "I could tell."

Jessie's jaw dropped. That almost sounded like Loralee . . . was *jealous*. Of *her*? "But, he liked you more."

"Well, obviously." She tossed her hair back.

Jessie shook her head. She couldn't muster up the energy

to be angry with Loralee anymore. Besides, Max had made his choice. He could have told Loralee no, and he didn't.

"I'm on my way to see Ann-Marie." Loralee sniffed again. "What are *you* doing?"

Jessie wavered, then admitted, "I'm trying to find a spare key so I can break into Wes's house."

Loralee's eyebrows rose. "Interesting. Did you check under his flowerpots?"

"Obviously."

"Welcome mat? Window ledge? Large rocks? Under the stairs?"

Jessie scowled. "I did." She was seriously regretting telling Loralee anything.

"What about there?" Loralee pointed.

"Where?" Jessie frowned, trying to follow, but all she saw was Wes's tea mug and . . . "Oh, for the love of dog," she whispered.

Loralee snorted, then put a hand over her face. "I'm sorry. I promised I'd be nicer, but seriously, Jessie? You make it almost impossible not to make fun of you."

But for once, Jessie didn't care. Loralee could make fun of her all she wanted, because Jessie was pretty sure she'd just discovered the spare key's hiding spot. Right there in plain sight. She walked up the three steps to the front porch, picked up the empty mug, and flipped over the coaster.

And there it was, dull and burnished and unmistakably a key.

CHAPTER 34

Jessie crept back down the stairs, the key gripped so hard in her hand it was shaking.

"Well? Aren't you going to use it?" Loralee asked. "Also, why do you want to break into Wes's house? He's such a weirdo." She paused. "Unique individual."

"Do you still want me to tell Max you're nicer?"

"Yes. I mean, just if it happens to come up."

"Why?"

Loralee grimaced. "No reason."

Jessie stared at her, at this new, sadder, less-glossy version, and she realized, "*He* broke up with *you?*" So much for Ann's theory that Loralee would get tired of Max first. Had he ditched Loralee because she was so mean? Mean to *her?* Jessie's heart beat a little faster, and she remembered how he'd tried to apologize, to explain . . . but it didn't matter. He could break up with Loralee a hundred times and it wouldn't make up for what he'd done.

Loralee's nostrils flared. "Boys don't break up with me," she snapped. "It's just a misunderstanding. He'll get over it."

Jessie looked down at the key in her hand and up at

Wes's house. She had a plan, but she needed Loralee's help. Jessie shook her head. What was the world coming to when a person needed to rely on Loralee? This was all Wes's fault. He'd stolen Hazel, and that had thrown everything off. It was like Jessie's whole life had become a picture that was just a little out of focus. Sighing, she said, "If you do me one favor, just one small favor, then I'll tell Max how much nicer you've been."

"Really?" Loralee said. "You'd do that?"

"I would," Jessie said reluctantly, and then she told Loralee the plan. A dog's future was at stake, and that was more important than her revenge on Loralee, or Max's cute fox smile, or anything else.

Knock, knock, knock.

Jessie waited around the back of the house. It felt weird not being the one knocking at Wes's door for once, but she had to admit Loralee had the knocking down much better. Somehow, when Loralee knocked, it sounded demanding and impatient, like you'd better answer that door, or else. Even Wes wouldn't be able to resist.

"Go away, kid," Wes hollered.

"Mr. Kowalski?" Loralee asked, her voice loud enough to carry to the back of the house. "Mr. Kowalski, I need to speak with you."

Jessie heard the sound of the front door opening and the mumble of voices. She had to act, and fast.

Carefully, she fit the key into the lock of the back door, turned it, and eased the door open. Then she crept inside Wes's house.

He still had all the blinds drawn, but there was a light on next to his chair in the living room. She saw a throw blanket and a book, but no dog. Frowning, Jessie slipped further into the house, glad she was out of sight from the entryway. She glanced at the kitchen up ahead, then turned right, went down a short hall, and stopped in front of a closed door. She hesitated for just a second and then opened it.

She blinked, waiting for her eyes to adjust to the dim light filtering in, for the shapes in front of her to resolve themselves into a bed and a dresser. And there, in the far corner . . . a kennel.

Jessie hurried forward and opened the door. Hazel lifted her little snout.

"*Shh, shh*, don't do it," Jessie whispered, petting the dog. "Don't howl." She picked Hazel up, then slipped out of the room and crept toward the back door. She was so close. She reached for the doorknob.

" . . . not going to buy anything, you hear me? Now go away." Wes slammed the front door.

Hazel let out a loud, long howl.

Jessie's heart stopped beating and then slammed faster into her rib cage to make up for missed time. She grabbed the door handle and turned it just as Wes flew into the room. She froze, half in and half out of the house.

Wes's eyes were wide, but he just stood there. "Don't," was all he said, before Jessie turned and ran out of the house, Hazel secure in her arms. She sprinted all the way down the stairs and back into the street, but Wes never caught her. He didn't even try.

"Whoa, did you just steal a dog from him?" Loralee asked.

"Thanks for your help, gotta run!" Jessie called as she zipped past Loralee.

"Oooowooooo," Hazel sang, squirming.

"Don't forget your promise!" Loralee yelled after her.

Jessie ran down the street as fast as she could with an increasingly irritated dog in her arms. It seemed to take forever, but eventually she got to Hazel's house, and her steps slowed, then stopped.

She stared up at the brick front. It looked bigger today, more intimidating, and Jessie realized she had no idea what to do. Should she just ring the doorbell? Tell Diana she found her dog? Wait and see if Wes showed up and stopped her?

Why hadn't he shown up to stop her? He had to know what she was going to do.

"Oowoo?"

"I know, Hazel. It's your home," Jessie whispered, giving Hazel's wolfy head a quick kiss.

"Jessie?"

Jessie turned. "Oh. Um, hi Monique."

Monique looked terrible. Her hair was coming out of its braids, her eyes were red and swollen, and even Jessie could tell that her clothing didn't match. Purple should not be worn with orange. "Oh my god, Jessie, did you find her?" Monique stumbled closer, her hands reaching for Hazel.

Jessie wasn't sure what to do, so she let Monique take the dog.

Monique's whole face crumpled, and she hugged Hazel to her chest, her shoulders shaking. And Jessie realized:

Monique was crying. Not just a few tears but full body sobbing. Jessie felt awful, like she'd swallowed a whole jar of spiders.

"Oh, thank you, thank you," Monique sobbed, wiping her face on her sleeve. "I've been searching everywhere. I thought maybe she'd show up somewhere near her house, so I've been circling here, too. I just, I feel so, so bad." She sniffed. "I'm getting out of the biz. You can tell Wes. I'm done. I d-don't deserve to b-be a dog walker." Her eyes teared up again and she thrust Hazel back at Jessie, then walked away.

"*Ooowoo.*" Hazel stared at Jessie with those big brown eyes, and for once Jessie didn't see entitlement in them. She saw accusation.

Jessie bit her lip. The spiders in her stomach grew until she thought she might be sick. This was what she'd wanted. This was what she'd been working for. Monique out of the business, Wes back, everything the way it was supposed to be, right? Then why didn't it feel right?

Her fault.

Jessie had done this to Monique. She had sabotaged Monique's business, had stolen her key, had set Wes up to take Hazel. It all led back to Jessie.

Jessie was a meaner person than Loralee could ever hope to be.

CHAPTER 35

Diana opened her door slowly, her eyes staring through Jessie.

"*Owoooooo! Ooooowooooo!*" Hazel squirmed free from Jessie's arms and leapt straight at Diana, who caught her midair.

"H-Hazel? Hazel!" Diana laughed and hugged the pup like she'd never let her go again while Hazel howled and bathed Diana's face in wolfy kisses. When Diana finally set her down, Hazel danced around her feet, curled tail wagging, and something inside Jessie softened. This was right. This felt right.

Then Diana hugged her, which didn't feel right at all. "You found her. Thank god you found her." She squeezed Jessie like a juice box before finally letting her go. "I am so sorry I ever switched from Wes. That Monique is terrible, and I never should have listened to her. Isn't that right, Hazel?" Diana crouched down and scratched Hazel behind the ear, her expression hardening. She reminded Jessie of a battle-ax, all steel and sharp angles. "I'm telling everyone." Diana straightened.

"No one is going to want Monique to walk their dogs anymore."

Jessie swallowed hard. She thought of Monique crying over Hazel, so relieved she'd been found. Then she thought of Wes, of how broken he'd been when all his dogs had started leaving him. If she told the truth, Monique's reputation would be cleared . . . but Wes's would be ruined.

Jessie clutched the banister next to her. She felt dizzy.

"Are you OK, honey? Do you want something? Maybe something to eat or drink? And of course, there's the reward money. Truly, I can't even tell you how grateful I am."

Jessie closed her eyes. She was the worst. The absolute worst. "N-no. You sh-shouldn't be grateful." Her tongue felt huge and swollen. She imagined Angel's tongue lolling out of her own mouth, and somehow that gave her the courage to continue. Calm, confident energy. She opened her eyes, looked Diana full in the face. "It was my fault. Not Monique's."

"What?" Diana blinked. "What do you mean?"

"I stole your dog."

Diana went still. "You? Stole? My dog?" she managed, her voice shaking.

"Y-yes." Some of Jessie's borrowed confidence deserted her, and she inched backward on the top step.

"Why? Why would you do that?"

"Because . . . because . . . I didn't think you deserved her." Now that the words had started, they just flooded right out of Jessie's mouth. "You leave Hazel with Wes all the time, and Wes loves her, and she loves him, and everyone was happy. But then you took her away from him for your own selfish reasons. You didn't care what was best for Hazel, and it totally crushed Wes, so . . . so I took her. So you'd see what it feels like."

Diana's eyes were so wide the whites showed all around them.

Jessie took a step back, her heel hanging off the edge of the top step. "But," she whispered, suddenly empty, "I brought her back. Because she missed you. And I'm sorry."

"You're sorry? You're *sorry*?" Diana screeched. "Get off my porch, you horrible child! I don't know what Wes was thinking, letting you help him, but you can bet he won't let you near any of his dogs now."

Jessie staggered back as if struck. She hadn't considered that, but, of course, Wes wouldn't be able to let her help anymore. She was a known dognapper now, public enemy number one to the canine nation. She'd never be able to walk dogs here again.

CHAPTER 36

J essie?" Ann asked softly. "Jessie, are you OK?"

"I'm great," Jessie said into her pillow. "I'm never getting out of bed again, but I'm great." After dinner yesterday, her aunt had gotten a phone call. Someone told her all about Jessie stealing a dog. Of course, then her father had to be told, and Jessie was forced to suffer through a very depressing phone call home in which he said it seemed like she wasn't ready for the responsibility of having a dog of her own. When it was over, she'd gone to bed and hadn't moved since.

Now that she was awake, she could tell Saturday morning was going to be beautiful. Already, sunlight was doing its best to filter in through Ann's curtains. Traitorous sunlight. It didn't belong here.

"Jessie, you could just tell the truth," Ann said. "We both know you didn't steal Hazel. Wes did."

"No," Jessie said. "I'm taking that secret to the grave with me. And so are you. You promised, Ann-Marie."

Ann winced. "Just Ann, please."

Jessie blinked. "Really?"

Ann shrugged. "It sounds weird when you say it."

"It sounds weird when anyone says it. Marie is just your middle name."

"I know."

Jessie turned back to her pillow.

"Jessie," Ann sighed.

"Go away."

"You can't just hide up here forever."

"I can hide here for another week. Then Dad will pick me up, and I'll find a new place to hide." Jessie could feel Ann hovering, wanting to say more, but in the end, she left her alone. *Good*, Jessie thought. She deserved to be alone. If it weren't for her, none of this would have happened.

She thought of her future dog, the dog she'd never have now, and buried her face harder into her pillow.

Jessie wasn't sure how long she lay like that. She'd planned to lay there forever, but eventually, she really had to pee. And then once she was up, she realized how hungry she was. And then after she ate, she felt too restless to just lay in bed. Ann was out, probably reuniting with Loralee, so Jessie just wandered listlessly around the house until Uncle David stopped her.

"Haven't seen you with this thing in a while," he said, holding up her soccer ball. "Maybe it's about time you took it for a spin?" He tossed it at her.

Jessie caught it automatically. "I don't know . . ." she began.

"I don't think Veronica is taking the summer off of soccer practice."

"Vanessa," Jessie said automatically, thinking of her

old soccer rival. That all seemed so far away and long ago. Still, she found herself walking to the park, her soccer ball tucked under one arm. She might as well do some solo drills. It wasn't like she had anything better to do. And at least that was one good thing about not getting a dog; she'd have plenty of time to keep training.

When she got to the park, she stretched and began warming up. A few minutes later, Max showed up. Jessie wasn't surprised. Half of her had been expecting him to be there already. She *was* surprised, however, when he walked over. He had to have heard about her theft of Hazel. He probably hated her as much as she used to hate him. Because she realized, as she watched him, that she didn't hate him anymore. She was too sad for that. Now when she looked at him, she felt nothing at all.

"Hey, Jess." He stopped a few feet away from her, then took off his hat and turned it backward.

"What do you want?" Jessie asked.

"To play you in soccer." Max grinned. He still had a cute smile, but looking at it didn't make Jessie's stomach flutter anymore. "Look, I know you didn't steal that dog. I might be stupid, but I'm not that stupid."

"I don't think you're stupid. Well, maybe a little stupid," she amended. "I mean, you were dating Loralee . . ."

He winced.

Jessie thought about her enemy and sighed. "Speaking of, she has been *a lot nicer* lately."

Max's eyes widened. "Really?"

"I guess so."

An awkward silence stretched between them.

"Jessie, I'm sorry," Max finally said. "I think you're really fun, and funny, and I liked being your friend. I'm sorry I ruined that."

"I'm sorry, too. About your mom. And Hazel. And everything."

"Here's an idea . . ." he said slowly, carefully, like he was walking on a tightrope over boiling lava. "How about we play for it? If I beat you, we forget about the stupid things I did and start over?"

Jessie thought about it. She remembered how hurt she'd been, learning that Max was just getting information out of her. Or all the times she'd planned to meet him at the park and he'd stood her up. But she also remembered how much fun she'd had playing soccer with him. Did she want to be friends? She chewed her lip. Wes was right; everyone did leave you eventually. But sometimes they came back. Like Ann. Ann, who had ended up being there for her when she really needed it.

But Max? She'd already forgiven him, again and again. What had he done to earn yet another chance? She looked at him, at this boy she'd thought of all summer. "You know what's great about dogs?" she asked.

Max blinked. "What?"

"They are so very forgiving. But even though I want to be a dog, I can't be. No matter how many Rules I master." Even as she said those words, she realized the truth: Despite Wes's claim, the Rules of the Ruff would never teach her how to be a dog. But maybe they'd taught her a little something about how to be a person.

Max tilted his head, confusion filling his big brown eyes.

Jessie felt calm and confident. She was aware of her surroundings, both inside and out. And this time, she knew when to leave it. "Good-bye, Max," she said. "Maybe next summer, I'll play you. But for now, I think I'd rather drill alone."

She turned and walked away.

CHAPTER 37

Jessie spent the rest of the week drilling on her own in the park and hanging out with Ann. Occasionally, she even spent time with Loralee, who was still doing her best to be "civil." Unfortunately, Loralee's best wasn't really all that good, but by now Jessie could see the end of summer looming, and it didn't really matter.

And while Jessie did miss her dog friends, she also realized how nice it was to focus on soccer and not have to worry about getting them out. And she definitely didn't miss all the poop scooping. In a lot of ways, life was much easier now.

Sometimes she'd see Wes or Monique walking dogs in the distance, but they never approached her, and she never went up to them, either; whenever she thought about visiting Wes, she'd remember the hurt in his eyes when she took Hazel back, and she just couldn't.

But the day before she was supposed to go home, she finally gathered up all her courage and went over there.

Jessie couldn't help remembering all the times she'd stood here on this doorstep, just like this. And as she knocked, she felt the echo of those other times vibrating beneath her fist.

Wes slowly opened his door. "I wondered when you'd be by."

Jessie shrugged. "I just, I came to say good-bye. And to return this." She held out her purple hip pack, but Wes didn't move to take it.

"That's yours, kiddo. You earned it fair and square."

"But I'm not a dog walker anymore."

"Did you learn the Rules of the Ruff?"

"I think so," Jessie said.

"Then you're a dog walker. You'll always be a dog walker. In here." He tapped his heart, then pointed at hers.

For some reason, that made her feel much better. She slung her hip pack over her shoulder. "I figured it out, by the way," she said. "The real meaning behind the Rules. They're not just for dealing with dogs."

Wes frowned. "What are you talking about? Of course, they're just for dogs."

"And people." Jessie grinned proudly, but Wes's frown was like marble. "Right?" she asked, some of her certainty leaking away.

"Listen, kid, I wouldn't waste my time making up rules for dealing with people."

"You . . . made them up?" she whispered.

"Obviously I made them up. Where did you think they came from? Did you think they were some ancient dog-walker wisdom passed down through the ages?"

Jessie squirmed. That was exactly what she'd thought. "No," she lied.

Wes laughed and slapped his knee. "You know, I never thought I'd say this, but I'm going to miss having an assistant."

"Good luck getting another one," Jessie grumbled. Was everything he'd taught her a lie?

But then she thought back to all the times the Rules had helped her. Maybe . . . maybe they really *were* ancient dog-walker wisdom, only he wasn't allowed to admit it. That made a lot more sense than the idea that Wes had just invented them all summer.

"Anyhow, kid, I'm actually glad you came by," Wes said, his good humor fading. "I wanted to say thanks. Not just for being my assistant but for doing the right thing when I couldn't."

Jessie froze. "You mean . . . Hazel?"

"Of course I mean Hazel. I don't know what I was thinking." His shoulders slumped. "I've already talked to Diana, by the way. Admitted the whole thing."

"You *what?*" Here Jessie had covered for him, and he'd gone and told the truth anyhow?

"I had to. A dog wouldn't have lied like that." He sighed. "Besides, Diana deserved the truth." He tapped the door frame idly, like his fingers were moving in time with his thoughts.

"Is she still going to let you watch Hazel?" Jessie asked quietly.

Wes's fingers stilled. "No," he said, just as quietly. "No, that's pretty much done."

Jessie nodded. She wanted to cry, but this sadness inside her was too heavy for tears. It reminded her of when her dad talked about *before*, and then stopped suddenly, her mother's name hanging unspoken around them. Jessie wanted to ask what her mother had been like when she was younger, wanted to see pictures of her from their wedding, hear stories about how they met. But her tongue was always burdened then by the same weight she felt now.

Still, at least she had her dad, and her dad had her. Wes really would be alone now. Even if he had all his other dogs again, without Hazel . . .

"Did I tell you Diana and I used to work together?" Was asked suddenly.

Jessie shook her head.

He smiled. "We were hired together. Back in my old life, before Sarah . . . well." He sighed. "She kept in touch when I left the engineering firm, when my life fell apart. I'm still not sure why, what she sees . . . what she saw in me."

"Are . . . are you getting back together with your ex-wife?"

Wes shook his head. "We have dinner together every year on the anniversary of our divorce. It's a miserable tradition, but it makes Sarah happy." He frowned. "Apparently it didn't make Diana very happy. Ah well. It's for the best. Relationships are too messy. Take my advice, kid, and stay far away from them. In fact . . ." He pulled something small and round out of his pocket and tossed it at Jessie. "That's for you."

She caught it, startled. It was the size of the palm of her hand and heavier than it looked. A magnet, white with familiar maroon letters. "Dogs. Because People Suck."

"If I've taught you nothing else this summer, I'm sure I've taught you that." He tilted his head and smiled at her. "But maybe not *all* people."

"Thank you." Jessie clutched the magnet closer to her.

Wes nodded, then closed the door in her face, but gently for once.

CHAPTER 38

Honk! Honk!

"That's my ride." Jessie grinned and shouldered her backpack and duffel.

"I'll walk you out," Ann said.

"Hey, hey, there's my girl!" Jessie's dad called when he saw her. Jessie squealed and dropped her bags, then flew forward to give him a big hug. She'd almost forgotten how tall her dad was, and how solid he felt as he picked her up and swung her around.

"I missed you," she said.

"I missed you, too, Jess." He set her down and kissed the top of her head, then laughed as Ann struggled over with the dropped bags. "Thanks, Ann. You keeping out of trouble?"

"Always, Uncle James."

"Unlike my daughter, eh?"

Jessie winced. She was hoping she could tell her dad the truth about everything later, once she'd left Elmsborough far behind. She didn't really want to discuss it now.

"Look at that face," her dad laughed, tapping her on the chin. "I have just the thing to wipe that expression clean off." He opened the back seat and pulled out . . .

"A kennel?" Jessie felt like there was no air in her lungs, or maybe too much air. "A . . . dog kennel?"

Grinning, her dad opened the kennel, and pulled out a little black-furred dog, one with pointed ears and a white snout and the biggest, brownest eyes Jessie had ever seen. With the exception of one dog.

Jessie dropped to her knees, and her dad put the pup in her arms.

"*Ooowooo?*" The pup snuffled at her face with a little wolfy snout.

"A Klee Kai? You got me a Klee Kai?"

"Cutest dog ever, eh?"

Jessie hugged her dog, laughing as the pup squirmed and licked her on the face. Her heart felt so big right now, so full. She pictured it as the ocean, the world, the universe. "I thought you said I wasn't ready for a dog."

"We-ell," her dad said, "I got a phone call the other day. Some guy named Wes."

"Wes called you?"

"He sure did. Apparently there aren't that many James Jamisons out there, so I was easy to find. He told me he had to set the record straight." Her dad crouched down beside her. "And he did. Honey, I think you might not have done the best thing, but you did what you thought was right, and you accepted the consequences of your actions. I'm so proud of you." He ruffled her short hair.

Jessie sniffed and looked down at her new pup, her eyes blurring. "What's her name?"

"Whatever you want it to be." He paused. "Originally, though, her name was Rosi."

"Rosi." Jessie studied the pup. "Rosi Ruff," she decided.

"Nice alliteration." Her dad beamed.

Jessie's heart squeezed. She looked at her new dog. A dog who would need a lot of time, and attention, and love. Was she really ready to give all of that up? And not just for a walk or two?

"What's this?" Her dad picked something up off the ground. "Hmm. Nice magnet. Not sure I agree with the sentiment, though."

Jessie glanced down. Her dad was holding the magnet Wes had given her; it must have fallen out of her pocket when she picked up Rosi. She looked at him, at the smile lines around his eyes, the mustache in need of a trim, the baggy basketball T-shirt he wore, so similar to her own, and she knew Wes had it all wrong: Some people never left you.

She took the magnet back from her dad and understood what she had to do.

Five minutes later, she'd said good-bye to Ann and was on her way.

"Are you sure about this?" her dad asked, frowning.

"I'm sure. I'm sorry, Dad, but I'm sure."

They parked, and Jessie got out of the car, Rosi's kennel clutched firmly in both hands. She knocked at Wes's door, one final time.

He opened it, his eyes widening. "Jessie?" He looked out at the car, where Jessie's dad was waiting.

"You taught me the first five Rules of the Ruff," Jessie said quickly. "But I also learned a sixth Rule." She took a deep breath. "All dogs come into your life for a reason."

Wes frowned down at her. "What do you mean?"

She thrust the kennel at him, and he took it automatically.

"What's this?" he asked.

"Open it."

Already, Rosi was getting antsy in there, poking her nose out. "*Ooowooo?*"

Wes's fingers shook as he set the kennel down, opened it, and picked Rosi up and held her. "What's her name?"

"Rosi Ruff."

Wes grinned. "Terrible alliteration."

Jessie swallowed. "That's exactly what I thought you'd say," she whispered. She took a deep breath, then said the words. "She's yours."

Wes's grin faded. He stared at her.

"Someone once told me that owning a dog is a big responsibility. I think you're ready for that now." Jessie reached forward and ran a finger down Rosi's little wolfy head. "Take good care of her."

She took a step back, then another. Wes stood there, frozen, the pup in his hands, but he didn't try to give her back, and after a minute, Jessie knew he wasn't going to. He would keep her and give her a better home than Jessie could. The best home. And in return, Rosi would make sure he wasn't alone anymore.

She turned to go, then stopped. "You know, you might consider working with Monique."

Wes blinked. "What?"

"I mean, you're much better with dogs than she is, but she's pretty good with the other stuff. The people stuff. You could team up."

Wes scowled. "I work alone."

"You worked with me all summer. It wasn't so terrible, was it?"

His expression softened. "I guess I did kind of get used to having an assistant."

Jessie knew that was the best she was going to get, so she left him there, cradling his new dog.

She would get her own dog someday; she was sure of it. Just as she was sure dogs, like people, really did come into your life for a reason.

As she watched Elmsborough drop away in the car window, she thought of everything she'd learned, both the big Rules and the little tricks Wes had taught her. "You know, there are probably lots of dogs in our new neighborhood, right?" she said.

"Uh-huh," her dad replied absently.

"Dogs that need walks?"

"What are you thinking?" he asked slowly.

"I'm thinking . . . I might want to start my own business." And she gave him her very best smile. The one that wore down stones and filled oceans.

Acknowledgments

My two favorite things in all the world are dogs and writing, and I owe a million thanks to my husband, Sean Lang, who first suggested combining the two, and to all my GoDogz, who taught me the Rules of the Ruff. Also to the Santa Cruz dog-walking community—thank you for being so welcoming and supportive.

A huge shout-out to Ben Baxter, Jessie's very first fan, and Jennifer Azantian, the best agent a girl and her dog story could hope for. Also thank you to my wonderful editors, Erica Finkel and Masha Gunic. All of you helped shape this story in ways I never could have imagined, and I am forever grateful for all your feedback and support.

To the rest of the team at Abrams who helped make this book a reality: Alyssa Nassner, Josh Berlowitz, Kyle Moore, Tessa Meischeid, Nicole Schaefer, Jenny Choy, Melanie Chang, Andrew Smith, Jody Mosley, Mary Wowk, Elisa Gonzalez, and Rebecca Schmidt; thank you so much for all the hard work you put into this. Also to Julia Bereciartu, for your delightful illustrations.

Thank you to all the wonderful writers who have helped along the way, including Alan Wehrman, Moanna Whipple, and Teresa Yea, my awesome beta readers, as well as Miles Zarathustra, Colleen Smith, Meg M., and Joan McMillan, the rest of my tremendous critique group. And to my family: my parents, Rich and Rose; my in-laws, Lyn and Bruce; my sisters, Kati and Rosi; and my brothers, Nick, Ed, and Jesse, I'm glad you're all part of my pack.

And finally, to all my fellow dog walkers, who know how impossibly hard and endlessly rewarding this job can be—this one's for you.